To Sherex

My Time in the Sun

a novella and memoir
by Naleighna Kai

Peace + Joy

Macro Publishing Group
Chicago, Illinois

Macro Publishing Group
Macro Marketing & Promotions Group
888.854.8823
www.macrompg.com

My Time in the Sun ©2016 by Naleighna Kai
Special Edition

Cover design: J. L. Woodson for Woodson Creative Studio
                    www.jlwoodson.com
Editorial Team: Janice Pernell janice.pernell@gmail.com
                    www.janicepernell.com

Interior Book Design: Lissa Woodson of www.naleighnakai.com

Macro Publishing Group special edition - October 2016

Manufactured and Printed in the United States of America

My mother, Jean Woodson
My grandmother, Mildred E. Williams
My brother, Eric Harold Spears
My niece, LaKecia Janise Woodson,
a shooting star who left us much too soon

Anthony "Green Eyes" Johnson, the man who helped me learn
what unconditional love is all about.

To Leslie Esdaile Banks (L.A. Banks), one of the best
storytellers the planet had to offer. Thank you for your
encouragement, advice, and uplifting words.
You are missed more than I can say.

To Octavia E. Butler, an author who created that wonderfully
dynamic kind of literary work that will live on forever.

In loving memory of my niece,
LaKecia Janise Woodson

Acknowledgments

All praise is due to the Creator first and foremost. A special love and respect to my guardian angels, ancestors, teachers and guides.

To my mother Jean Woodson, to my true mother, Sandy Spears, and my mentoring mother, Bettye Mason Odom; to my son, Jeremy "J. L." Woodson, who is even still, my blessing. To the people who continuously inspire me: Rev. Renee "Sesvalah" Cobb-Dishman, Jennifer Cole-Addison, DeMarco Suggs, Janine Ingram, Martha Kennerson, Keshia Cee, Pam Nelson, Sharon Lucas, Louise L. Hay, Debra Mitchell, Ehryck F. Gilmore, Lorna "L.A." Lewis, Pastor Karen Williams To my editorial team and best friend: Janice Pernell.

To the readers who purchased this special edition copy ... I can't thank you enough for continuing to support me.

Enjoy!

Chapter 1

November 2004

"I cut him until I felt better."

The words, in their chilly delivery, caused an icy silence to descend on the police interview room.

Seconds ticked by before a blonde officer whispered, "Everyone, out."

Two uniformed men had been the first to arrive on the scene at a penthouse in the heart of downtown Memphis, where the man called "Daddy" housed a stable of teens that serviced clients with an array of wicked tastes.

Those officers gave one last lingering look at Kari and a glaring one at the blonde before trudging toward the door. When it closed behind them a ring of finality lingered that would only be matched by that of prison bars clanging shut, separating her from the outside world. Yes, that was what she had to look forward to because …

I cut him until I felt better

Flashes of his blood spreading on the faded carpet echoed in the corners of her memory. His gasp of surprise, eyes widened in shock, mirrored the horror she felt over the action she'd taken to protect one who could not protect herself. After two years within Daddy's clutches, sixteen-year-old Kari Mason had done whatever it took to ensure that her nightmare would finally end and someone else's would never begin. All it took was the appearance of another innocent to incite her to do the one thing that would stop her suffering and others.

"Tell me what happened," the officer commanded, sliding a half-filled notepad to the other side of the metal table. Then she went to a console and switched off the speaker that allowed those on the opposite side of the mirrored glass to listen in.

"Don't I need a lawyer?"

She took hold of Kari's upper arm, holding it firmly but not roughly, guiding her to a chair with its back to the glass. "Sit," she commanded, nodding toward the seat. "Tell me what happened," she insisted, blue eyes flashing with some type of unfamiliar emotion; thin pink lips pressed into a hard line.

Kari closed her eyes for a moment, summoning any ounce of strength she had left. Most of it had abandoned her the moment she saw Daddy for the monster he was. The moment she realized she had left the safety of her parents' household and traveled nine hundred miles with a predator who had every intention of using her until she died. And they all died at some point. She stopped counting after the first nineteen.

"I disobeyed him," Kari said. "And this time he was going to send me to the slicer."

"The slicer?"

"A john who specialized in killing a woman … one piece at a time."

The blonde swallowed, tried to keep her expression neutral, but when her gaze flickered toward the glass, Kari could tell she was familiar with that type of crime.

"I told Daddy I couldn't do it anymore. The men. So many of them.

Every day," she whispered in a voice that she barely recognized as her own. "I was tired. So, so, tired."

The tears came and she was surprised that she had any left to shed. She turned her face to the woman sitting across from her; a woman who had given her name but it still escaped Kari whenever she tried to remember. So she was just "the blonde" for now. "I was tired of not knowing what new thing they'd do to me. I was tired of men beating me, hurting me, doing all manner of whatever to me. Like I didn't matter. Like I was never somebody's something."

Kari wiped her tears with the back of a trembling hand. She felt dead inside. Had felt that way for a long time. "The slicer would have ended all of that for me. And I accepted that. But it wouldn't have helped the new girl Daddy brought in."

The blonde's gaze narrowed on Kari. "What was so different about her?"

"She's the youngest one," she replied, lowering her gaze to the remnants of her half-eaten meal as the image of the raven-haired child with expressive dark brown eyes came to mind. "She couldn't be more than ... six. Seven."

The blonde stiffened. A vein throbbed at her ivory temple, making Kari question if blood was still flowing through her own body.

"I was fourteen when I fell in love with Daddy," she confessed, clasping her hands to stop the trembling. "He wasn't like this in Chicago. He was .... nice. Kinder to me than my parents had been. I didn't know what he was. I didn't know men like him existed." She inhaled and let it out slowly as seconds ticked by and she was no closer to calm than when they first escorted her into this dim gray room. "But that child ... I ... I ..."

Kari looked away, focusing on the glass. She'd seen enough cop shows to know that even though the speaker had been turned off, an audience of people was looking in. But what did it matter? Her real life had ended the moment she slipped into the passenger seat of Daddy's car for what she thought would be a new adventure that would take her away from her strict mother and even stricter Bible-thumping father. So certain that the man in the driver's seat loved her more than he loved the other girls she'd seen him with over those few semesters. She'd felt so special then. He was Marquis Golden at that time. Only when they'd landed in a cheap motel in Memphis did the beginnings of the never-ending nightmare start.

"I'm your Daddy now," he'd said, and the punishment he exacted was far worse than anything her real daddy had ever done.

I cut him until I felt better ...

Chapter 2

"One mistake and I'm here," Kari said in a low tone, shame radiating from every pore. "I made *one* mistake and now I'm at a place so low that God can't even find me."

"Don't believe that," the blonde said in a hushed whisper, and for a moment Kari thought the woman wanted to say more. A police officer who'd probably seen things worse than Kari had ever laid eyes on was speaking of God in that manner?

"Look at me." Kari held her arms out in front of her letting the woman get a good look at a sampling of what she had endured. "Who's gonna love me like this?" she asked, more about the damage done to her soul than the bruises and welts on her body. "Who's gonna care about me? With the things I've done. With the things they made me do." She lowered her hands to the table, brittle nails once polished with an innocent pink blush now broken to the quick.

"At least I was lucky," she admitted, trying to find a shred of light in the darkness. "When Mindy got pregnant, he beat the baby right out of her. She lost that baby and her life. When Kimmie made a client angry by refusing to do something he asked, Daddy put a bullet in her knees and said she'd be perfect for clients who preferred a cripple." Kari lifted her head and locked gazes with the woman. "Bet you never thought there were men who wanted handicapped children. But there were. You can't imagine some of the things they wanted from us. I did whatever I had to do." She inhaled again; finding some balance, then let it out in a long stream. "I didn't care what happened to me, but that little girl ..."

"You listen to me," the blonde said, and this time she took Kari's hands in her own. They were soft, warm and the only touch she'd had in the last few hours. "First, you're wrong. God cares. Second, I'm going to need you to adjust your story a little."

Kari's head whipped toward the woman, taking in the furrowed brow, eyes the color of a morning sky, lips with a hard edge, and ivory skin that reddened with every mention of the child Kari had saved or hint of the danger she'd been in.

I cut him until I felt better ...

This woman had been the one who'd taken the knife from Kari's hand, then managed to have the decency to cover Kari's blood-splattered body with a sheet from the medical examiner's van when the crime lab had taken her clothes for evidence.

After they escorted her into this drab room with its dim lighting, the burly officers who'd vacated the room a while ago had wanted to withhold food and water until Kari gave a statement. The blonde refused. Soon there was a burger and fries, ginger ale, and a short period of time to feel human again. And an unfortunate silence that allowed the scenes of the evening to replay in startling clarity.

"You can't speak those words that you said when you first came in here," the blonde said with a wary glance toward the mirrored glass.

"But it's the truth."

"The truth is going to need a little adjustment," she replied slowly, as though willing Kari to understand something that she couldn't truly voice in the presence of the colleagues who were watching. "If you can testify to the things you've seen him do ..."

Kari's mind swirled a moment, trying to grasp what the officer was laying on the table. A faint ray of hope lit the corners of her mind.

"You saw that girl's body?" the blonde ventured. "The one he killed?"

"He didn't have a problem doing that in front of us," she replied. "Said it sent a message to the rest of us." She swallowed hard, trying to force the words around the lump that had formed in the center of her throat. "I was in the car when he dumped her. He was never afraid that we'd say anything." She shrugged, remembering some of the times she'd had the opportunity to attract the attention of someone she thought could help her. But she was never sure who would look at her and believe the things she had to say. Daddy's clients were some of the most normal looking people. "Besides, we were headed to a client nearby, so putting her in the ground on the way was convenient. Work comes first."

The blonde took the notebook and scribbled a few words. "Do you think you could lead us to where he put the body?"

Kari shifted her gaze to the nearest wall, her mind flickering through the progression of that night, zeroing in on a few landmarks that might be helpful. "I think so. He made me dig the grave. It was cold. The ground was hard. It took forever."

The blonde simply nodded as though this sort of talk was a normal thing. In her line of work, maybe it was.

"The minute this trial is over," the blonde said, "I'm going to personally put you on the bus to Chicago."

"There's nothing for me there."

"There's nothing for you here," the blonde countered.

She had a point. A damn good one.

I cut him until I felt better ...

"The more I know those fine Bible-toting and quoting never-did-anything-wrong-in-their-lives church folks, the more I believe Satan never had truer followers." – Naleighna Kai

Chapter 3

Chicago, Illinois
Twelve years later

All eyes were focused on the richly dressed man swaggering past the organ, down the plush maroon carpet of the center aisle, then the maple wood pews filled with morning worshippers.

"The first lady was a prostitute," Minister Henderson bellowed loud enough to carry the entire length of the sanctuary and echo from the cathedral ceilings. "A fourteen-year-old prostitute. Not the kind of woman we want our little girls and young women to emulate."

Aridell Henderson Jones stood up along with several others, as she said, "Get thee behind me Satan. And *stay* there."

Sam, the choir director, shouted, "Have you lost your cotton-picking, chicken-plucking mind? This isn't the place for that."

The silence was nothing short of mind-blowing. Slowly, murmurs became whispers. Those whispers became a collective voice. That collective voice became a roar of discontent so loud it might have been a scream that could break the stained-glass windows.

Kari Kimbrough's heart rate sped up to the point of nearly bursting out of her chest. She brushed a hand down her thighs to smooth out the lavender silk dress that draped her curvaceous frame. She glanced at her husband in the pulpit, noticing that he quickly sheltered his shock as he stood and moved to the edge of the dais.

His hand went up. Voices trickled back down to whispers, and then silence slowly descended once again.

"And you're saying this in front of the entire congregation hoping to achieve what, Minister Henderson?" Pastor Kimbrough challenged, his sun-kissed complexion flamed with angry color. "To somehow make me ashamed of my wife?"

For a split second, the confidence that had been so evident in Henderson's demeanor slipped. But only for a second. Because the church's board and deacons suddenly rounded him in what seemed to be a show of support. Kari keyed into their solemn expressions that didn't show one ounce of surprise. This was planned. Evidently a long time in the making.

The fire in Pastor Kimbrough's dark brown eyes would normally be enough to quell the most disruptive of people. But not Terrance Henderson. Ever since he'd been ordained to preach by some unnamed pastor in California where he once lived, the ambitious minister had his sights on being the pastor of the church founded by his great-great grandfather, the good Reverend Jacob Lee Henderson. The position of pastor had been held for four generations of Henderson men. That is, until a scandal with one of the parishioners forced Terrance Henderson's father to make an exit stage left—with teenage mistress in tow—long before the son of his wife had come of age to enter the pulpit.

A board of deacons and trustees had conducted a series of interviews and background checks, searching for a new pastor to lead the congregation. Overlooking a slightly flawed past, they'd deemed Anthony J. Kimbrough worthy to make the cut. If Kari had undergone the same rigorous scrutiny, they might have seen that she had a little baggage *and* a carry-on.

Pastor Kimbrough pinned his focus on Minister Henderson; his shoulders tense with conviction as he said, "This woman is not just my wife, she's my partner in helping people in this community find the God they stopped serving a long time ago. To find peace when there's so little of it in other aspects of their lives." He moved down the aisle until he was toe-to-toe with Henderson, towering over him by a few inches. "And you couldn't even come in a way that was decent and in order, like a board meeting. No, you took the coward's way and tried to shame her publicly in the middle of Sunday morning service."

The members, from the choir, musicians, all the way to the usher board were on their feet, some voicing their support of Pastor Kimbrough, but a surprising number of them siding with Henderson, and a good majority staying silent and watching the fireworks as though they couldn't believe something this scandalous would unfold in Sunday service right between prayer and scripture.

"And the First Lady hasn't stood up to say it isn't true," Henderson challenged with a haughty lift of his chin.

"That's because her husband's defending her honor and character," Sister Terry shot back. "And she's doing what a first lady should do— she's letting him."

Several choruses of "Amen" and "that's right, my sister" rang through the sanctuary.

The thing Kari had feared most was playing out right before her eyes, hurting the man she loved in a way she never wanted. At that moment, she wished she could vanish into thin air as Enoch had done when he went to be with the Lord. No natural death there. One minute he was, and then he wasn't.

The hard part about all this? Her husband didn't know anything about this fragment of her past. She had buried it so deep, even she couldn't remember the details. That was supposed to be a good thing.

Pastor Kimbrough brushed past Henderson and took a few moments to scan the faces of the members, whose focus was squarely on him.

"Which of you, male *or* female, has something in your past that you don't want to remember?"

He paused, waiting for someone, anyone to respond. When they didn't, he ventured forward, shifting past the communion table. "If it wasn't fornication and adultery, it was drugs and alcohol, or violence, or stealing. Or maybe you're so perfect that you haven't harmed one person in your life. But what about your offenses against God?" Kimbrough spread his hands. "Have you been pious and self-righteous? As they say, "so *heavenly*-minded that you're no *earthly* good"? Are you guilty of idolatry—making money, your pleasures, your ambitions, more important than God?" He scanned the congregation again. "Who among us is without sin?"

No one moved. Several people averted their gaze. Others lowered their heads, perhaps hoping their guilt wasn't written all over their faces. Then almost every one reclaimed their seats. Henderson, however, eased his way towards the group of men standing near the front pew—board members and deacons, while sending some type of signal their way.

"I could go on casting stones." Kimbrough's eagle-eyed gaze swept across everyone. "Because I'm sure to hit someone at some point."

They all seemed either lost in thoughts of their own pasts or focused on the present judgment of their first lady. It was hard to tell. Only a few people besides her husband had stood up for her when that filth poured out of Henderson's mouth. That did not bode well for their future at this church.

"We want God's grace and mercy on our own lives, but we're not so quick to extend it to others." Kimbrough sauntered forward as though undeterred by the strange vibe that hung heavily over the sanctuary. "Some of us are quick to turn up our noses and pass judgment when someone walks in here that doesn't meet with our approval. Then we turn right around and act like we're blind to everything that's happening in the streets around us because we don't want to get involved." He pointed to the wooden sanctuary doors. "The crime right outside this place is getting worse."

Kimbrough walked the aisle until he stood in front of Kari, who resisted the urge to reach for him, to find comfort in the one place she always had—his arms.

"People don't want to come in here and worship because too many folks up in here don't want to go out there and love. You're so busy being holy that you forget that the church isn't a haven for saints; it's a spiritual hospital for hurting people. It's the one place they ought to be able to come to find the way to best live their lives." He caressed his wife's face with a gentle stroke of his hand. "That goes for all people, not just saved folks. *All* people. No matter what their background. No matter what their past. There is neither bond nor free, male nor female. All are one in Christ Jesus. Doesn't the good book say 'I will draw all men unto me'?" Pastor smiled, though his green eyes still spoke to the seriousness of the moment. "*All*," he stressed.

"Yes, that's a good speech and *all*," Henderson countered with a dismissive wave as his group fanned out behind him. "And there might be some truth in *all that*. But our leader and his wife should be shining examples. You can't get around that."

Murmurs of consent and others of dissent echoed from almost every corner of the church. The sound seemed to take a little wind out of Kimbrough's sails. A handful of members in the pews and most of the choir glared openly at Henderson with disdain. They hadn't shifted a gaze to Kari or the pastor during the last unfortunate exchange.

Henderson charged forward, locking a direct gaze with Kimbrough. "The board and deacons who run this church speak for all of the members. And they want a Henderson at the helm; someone they've known all their lives. Someone who has a *spotless* background. Wife included."

The men behind him nodded vigorously, but the members exchanged speaking glances that spoke to the fact that they never said any such thing. No one else spoke up to support that statement, which seemed to anger Henderson to a point.

"My ten percent seems to be making a difference up in this joint," said a freckled, red-haired member of the usher board. "So I'm all right with who we've got in the pulpit."

A chorus of agreement rippled through the sanctuary.

"Is this what you want," Henderson yelled, making eye contact with each member within his range, but gesturing to the man leading the charge for not casting any stones in his wife's direction. "If you want Pastor Kimbrough and a *former prostitute* to be the people who lead us and our children, stand and be counted."

Aridell Henderson Jones stood, quickly followed by a group of about twenty others, then the entire choir, the director, the musicians and that sole usher board member. None of the other one hundred or so members stirred. Their silence said everything.

Kimbrough's lips lifted in a smile that masked the disappointment that only a wife could detect. "Thank you for your honesty," he said to those who'd remained seated.

Tony held up two fingers and smiled at his wife. She returned his gesture by slowly holding up seven fingers of her own.

Then he extended his hand to Kari and she grasped it, legs trembling in an effort to stay steady. "It's all right, love," he whispered, and this time his smile reached his eyes. "It's all right."

Henderson swaggered down the aisle, unfazed by the fact that a few of his own family members were among those who opposed him. "That's right, leave," he taunted. "You and your whore."

Kimbrough was at Henderson's throat in the moment it took to blink; his hand clasping the man's throat and cutting off the air supply. The members who had taken a stand with Kimbrough inched back, giving him a wide berth. A few of the deacons and board members rushed forward in an attempt to break up the tussle.

Sister Aridell blocked their path along with a few who were standing to the side of her. Including Sister Vera who held up her cane and inched closer so she could slap it against the head of anyone who tried to hurt Pastor Kimbrough.

"Call my wife a whore again," Kimbrough said through his teeth, tightening his grip. "And I'll break one of the commandments right here and right now."

"Tony!" Kari said, and his head snapped toward her. "Don't. Please don't. Let. Him. Go."

Kimbrough took a few seconds, then complied. Henderson slipped to the carpet; gasping for whatever breath he could suck in.

"I'm not leaving because of what you said," Kimbrough declared, glowering at the man on the carpet still struggling to steady his breathing. "I'm leaving because anywhere that my woman isn't welcome, is not a place I need to be."

"You'd better say that," Sister Martha shouted.

"That's right," Brother Sam chimed in. "Be down for your wife."

Sister Vera raised a power fist and said, "That's what I'm talking about."

Kimbrough gave them an affirming nod, then switched his focus to look at the members backing Henderson. "A good seventy-to-eighty percent of this congregation is women. And if he could do this to one woman, what's to keep him from doing it to you?" Kimbrough gave the minister a sad shake of his head. "I was a man long before I accepted the call to the ministry. And any man worth his salt won't stand for any woman to experience what you've just done."

Kimbrough held out his hand and Kari rushed to his side. Then he looked over his shoulder at the mocha woman with salt-and-pepper sister locs down her back. The proud bearing in her stance spoke to her many years of experience and ability to overcome challenges that most didn't live to tell about.

"You coming, Sister Aridell?"

"When you think you're airing my dirty laundry for the entire world to see, don't be upset when I hang your drawers on the clothesline right next to mine." -- Naleighna Kai

Chapter 4

"We'll be on a little later, Pastor," Aridell Henderson Jones said, keeping a steely gaze on her youngest nephew before shifting that focus to Pastor Kimbrough. She waggled a finger toward him and Kari. "Y'all got some things to talk about since Junior Flip went running his mouth." She grimaced as she looked at Henderson once again and said, "The only time your mouth ain't doing some damage is when you're putting food in it or waiting for it to come out the other end."

Snickers and then outright laughter abounded from the congregation, causing Henderson's golden skin to flush a bright red. The tension eased in the sanctuary.

"I'm a grown man," he snarled, hands clenched into fists. "You can't talk to me like that."

"I can talk anyway I needs to. Especially if I'm telling the truth and shaming the Devil." She glanced at the couple standing in the aisle holding hands. "Go on home, pastor. She needs you right now. This kind of thing is a tough pill for a woman to swallow. Thank God she's got a strong man like you to love her."

Applause rang out and eclipsed all other sound in the church as some stood to show their support.

Pastor Kimbrough nodded, pressed a kiss to his wife's delicate hand and led her toward the sanctuary's exit. The congregation watched their progression in silence, until the ones standing near the center aisle gave Pastor Kimbrough and his wife a few reassuring words and handshakes along the way.

The moment the pastor and first lady were out of earshot, Aridell motioned for a thin woman to come to her. The woman's attention snapped to Aridell, who said, "Sister Sandra, go downstairs and let Sister Janice know that children's church is going to run a little bit longer today."

The woman sprinted down the aisle and was out of sight in seconds.

Those who stood with Aridell when Henderson had put forth the challenge to those who backed the pastor and first lady now moved closer to Aridell. The choir and the musicians left the stand and spread out near them as a show of solidarity.

"You want some truth?" she said, hazel eyes blaring with anger at Henderson, whose scowl showed his discomfort. "You only want to get your tail in the pulpit 'cause it's convenient since your wife can't bring home the bacon. Now you want the church to take up where she left off. Not gonna happen on my watch."

A few of the members murmured behind that statement and curious whispers showed that some might be having second or third thoughts about what was really going on.

Henderson pursed his lips but didn't have the balls to take on the woman who stood before him.

"I've been a member here all my life and I've heard many a preacher bring the Word." She sauntered up the aisle toward the covered communion table where everyone could see her clearly. "But I'm here to tell you that if you're expecting folks to get saved off that dribble you preach, then I'll let you in on a little something." She leaned in as though ready to impart a well-kept secret. "'Cause of you, they're a lot closer to having a ringside seat by the fire next to Satan himself."

Low whistles and a few laughs showed that she'd hit the mark. The board members gathered near Henderson, followed by the deacon board. They might not have been able to protect him from getting his tail whipped by Pastor Kimbrough, but they sure seemed adamant about showing whose side they were on.

"Hendersons own this church," he challenged, fists shaking at her and signaling his righteous indignation. "I've been in this church since I was born."

"And looks like you've been on the Devil's side the *whooooole* time." She nodded towards the group of men behind him. "They can control you, and believe you me, that's they *only* reason they want to put you in charge. They've been giving Pastor Kimbrough a hard time ever since he said we need to take the Word to the streets and stop waiting for folks to come in here. I don't see nothing wrong with that. But them?" She pointed to the men who were scowling in her direction. With a quick onceover of each one of them, she added, "Yeah, I see what you're about. Shenanigans and simple stuff."

Aridell turned, swept a gaze across the members of the congregation, some of whom were still whispering amongst themselves, probably trying to decipher what all of this meant. "Y'all can ride shotgun with this fella if you want to. I know what he's about too. Used to change his dirty diapers."

Henderson's chest puffed up. "I'm not in diapers anymore."

"But you're still full of the stuff that fills 'em up," she shot back with an eyebrow raised.

Even those who were on his side laughed at that statement. He shot them a look that quickly silenced them.

"On that note, I'll take my leave," she said, dismissing him with a dramatic flourish of her hand. "Need to see a man about his church."

The choir and the rest of her group were poised to follow, but she couldn't go without a parting shot.

"What you've got behind you are those who talk a good game," she taunted with a sly grin. "The people I'm taking with me are ones willing to stand with Pastor Kimbrough. They're the ones willing to do the work. Let's see you make this church work off of what your "followers" have to offer. And you're gonna want a salary too? Pastor Kimbrough never took a dime from this church. All these years, him and his wife have been supporting themselves through their own businesses."

Henderson flinched as though she'd struck him.

"You didn't know that?" She laughed and the flighty sound of it caused those around her to smile. "If you're gonna take his place, let's see you do *that*."

Henderson sputtered until he could wrap his lips around the words, "The church is *supposed* to take care of the pastor. That's how it's done."

Aridell shook her head. "Yeah, that's what I thought. Care to open up your bankbook for us to see? Pastor Kimbrough does it every month when he pays his tithes." She looked over his shoulder to his group, which was focused on them and their revealing exchange. "Am I right, heathens?"

Some of them, though angered by what she'd called them, still nodded grudgingly.

"You want his spot?" she challenged, perching on the arm of the nearest pew. "Then let's see you match him action-for-action. This church is debt free. When we raised money to construct this new building, he had it built one section at a time. No mortgage, no loans. The church owns this building free and clear. *That's* the kind of pastor he is."

Aridell left her seat and moved forward, touching the shoulder of Sister Joyce.

"Single mothers needed men to mentor their children, so Pastor Kimbrough challenged the men of this congregation to do just that." She swayed up the aisle. "He put programs in place to help the members become debt-free. See, *he* understands that being a pastor is more than just getting up in the pulpit, wearing fancy suits." She entered the circle of people who supported her and the good pastor, then faced the congregation and spread her arms. "We're going to get things straight. So the pastor and our first lady will feel comfortable coming back. And it looks like we need to appoint a new board."

"You can't do that," Henderson yelled, backed by grunts of agreement from the current board and deacons. "There's due process to elect a board."

"You attacked Pastor Kimbrough's wife all Willy Nilly," she countered. "Y'all didn't give him no due process. Her either."

That silenced the men.

Aridell gave them a toothy grin, taking in the panic-stricken expressions on the faces of the board, deacons, and her nephew. "We're gonna get this here church under control. The *right* kind of control." She gestured for the choir members, musicians, and the group she would call the Faithful Few to take a seat. They filed into some of the empty spots and waited.

"Y'all need to decide what kind of church we're gonna be," Aridell challenged. "If y'all want to be the kind where we come strutting in our Sunday best looking all pretty and putting on a show, listening to our good choir and soaking in a few words from our good pastor, then going about your lives like you never set foot in this place … well this ain't gonna be the church for you."

She shifted her focus to a few of the women closest to her. "I'm gonna say something else. Every female up in here should've been on her feet when my nephew came at your first lady like that," she snapped, waggling a finger at them. "But y'all sat there and let him attack her virtue, all the while knowing that some of you churchgoing women ain't closed your legs since the doctor opened them."

Gasps rent the air. A few hands fluttered before landing on bosoms that ranged from "slight" to "my bra cup runneth over".

"What did she mean by that," Sister Jean asked a woman next to her.

"Means when the doctor first checked to see whether it was a girl or a boy," Sister Beverly answered—and she didn't use her inside voice, either.

Sister Jean's hand instantly went up to cover her mouth to stifle a laugh. Others didn't even bother. They laughed outright and couldn't seem to get themselves under control.

"Now you wanna sit in judgment of somebody else, like you got that right," Aridell said. "This ain't gonna be that kind of church. We're about to be a family. A *real* family who looks out for each other and takes care of our community. And if you're not up for the challenge"— she nodded toward the exit—"the door's that way. Make real good use of it."

Aridell waited a few spells to see if anyone would leave. None did.

"You got a lotta nerve talking about family," one brash woman said, getting to her feet.

Aridell's gaze narrowed, finding the woman's features were the familiar ones of Terrance Henderson's younger sister, Lisa. She was as round as he was dense.

Lisa maneuvered past the people on her pew until she was in the aisle near Aridell. "One of your great nephews passed away. I didn't see you nor anyone else from your side of the family at his service this past Saturday."

Silence again. Some of the Faithful Few and choir sighed and shook their heads. Some mumbled words that Aridell couldn't catch.

"Did that woman really try to come for Sister Aridell like that?" Sister Vera said loud enough for those closest to her to hear.

Brother Mark stood and pointed at Lisa. "That was way out of line."

"That's some shady business right there," another person chimed in.

"Tasteless at best," the choir director said. Nearly all the choir members nodded and voiced their agreement.

"They do have a point," Aridell said to her niece with a mild shrug.

"Those clueless people have no idea what's even going on," Lisa snarled, throwing an angry glance at those she thought had spoken against her. "So they don't get to have any opinions. Anyway, your actions speak way louder than your words." Lisa's double chin lifted and her lips spread in an ugly smile, showing crooked teeth that hadn't seen a dentist since the baby ones fell out. "You can talk about family all day long, *Sister* Aridell. But you can't hide the fact that there's one part of your family that you've ignored all this time."

"You really want to go there? Here? Now?" Aridell countered, her voice a lot calmer than she actually felt. "I can tell you're related to him," she said, nodding toward Terrance, who frowned. "So let me be square as the young folks say." She closed the distance between them in a few strides, facing the weave-wearing woman head-on. "When you think you're airing my dirty laundry for the entire world to see, don't be upset when I hang your drawers on the clothesline right next to mine."

"You marry the type of man that you can submit to. I'm not being led by anyone who's not being led by the spirit of God. Even Paul wrote, "Follow me as I follow Christ." Not simply, 'Follow me.'"

-- D.J. McLaurin

Chapter 5

Kari glanced at her husband, who hadn't spoken a word on the drive to their tri-level home in Olympia Fields. His hand would reach out and touch hers from time to time, offering silent comfort, but it still wasn't enough to dispel the anxiety that filled her heart.

All these years, she'd managed to keep her past firmly buried. Everyone had skeletons in their closet. Unfortunately, hers still had some flesh on them.

"You know what? I think Sister Aridell's the type of Christian I'd always want on my side."

Kari raised a questioning brown.

"She's the one you call after you've done some real damage," Tony said, smiling. "Because she'll say I've got a shovel and I know just the place to hide the body."

"And that's the Christian thing to do?"

"Lighten up, sweetheart," he said in a weary tone. "I'm trying to wipe that serious expression from your face. Like you're about to be sentenced to the electric chair."

Kari turned her head to look out at the traffic whizzing by and didn't respond.

Tony released a sigh.

"I knew something had happened," he said, over the radio-filtered sounds of Mary Mary telling the world about the God in them. "It didn't matter then and it doesn't matter now. We're going to be all right, baby. We're *always* going to be all right."

Those words, spoken so plainly, lifted Kari's spirits. But only a little.

When they walked through the doors of a home that he'd had built from the ground up, the calming colors in shades of purple, blues and creams along with the scent of citrus greeted them. And so did the fact that she now had to provide answers and wade through a part of her life that shadowed her existence.

The blonde officer, Nancy, had been uncharacteristically kind and encouraging in her support of Kari while they were trying to build a case and waiting to see if Daddy would live or die. He was part of a syndicate of child sex traffickers who'd rather have seen Kari dead than on the stand testifying to what she'd seen them do. But an even bigger issue surfaced when Daddy survived those multiple stab wounds; barely hanging on for nearly two months before he showed actual signs of real life.

After Daddy was released from the hospital and went straight into police custody, the syndicate believed that at some point he'd start talking. Then the strategically sound wall they'd built to keep law enforcement spinning their wheels would come tumbling down, one person at a time. They didn't think twice about putting out hits on him and Kari. Which is why the FBI had tucked Kari away in a safe house to be sure she lived until the trial, but mostly to force Daddy to cut a deal and give the names of the higher-ups and the clients that would break the case wide open.

When Daddy realized that the syndicate had been unsuccessful in their several attempts to "take care of" Kari, and he would become their next target, he did what any non law-abiding citizen would do. He started singing. And it wasn't church hymns, either.

Thankfully, Nancy kept her promise and it was the only reason Kari had a good enough head start to get her life together when she made it back to the Windy City. After that, Kari was on her own.

The FBI and other law enforcement agencies had not been exactly shocked at the volume of children Daddy alone had managed to bring in. But they were appalled at the number of teens no longer on this side of the grave that Kari identified as having been part of the market. Children were a valuable commodity to Daddy, but they also weren't in short supply. Neither were the clients, which Kari later found were as high up as judges sitting in local courtrooms and as low as fathers with menial careers who had children of their own.

The only difference between Daddy's stable of teens and that of others who also had a house of girls was that most of his came from households with parents that loved them. Households like Kari's, where the adults' only sin was being too strict, maybe not letting them have friends from school or spend every waking hour watching television, or listening to secular music. Yes, those were grave sins in Kari's book at that time. She hadn't realized that there was a difference between a sin and an outright shame. Daddy taught her that. His clients taught her even more.

"I need you to understand that I love you unconditionally."

Her husband's voice jarred her back to her current reality. She had brought down a world of shame on a man she'd come to love more than life itself. The pain hit her all at once and so did a blinding rush of tears. She tried to run from the dining room, made it as far as the kitchen door, but he caught her up in his arms and said, "No, baby. You're not going to hide from this."

The words were gentle, but firm. So was his hold on her. "I had always hoped to be the kind of man that you could trust with your secrets. Remember when I first showed you my rap sheet?" he asked, stroking his hands down her back. "You told me then you wouldn't hold my past against me if I wouldn't hold yours against you."

Transparent. Kind. Loving. Gentle. He had always been that way, from the first time they met at a Jamaican restaurant. Kari remembered that day clearly. It was one that would change her life forever.

Kari walked into Jerk Heaven on the Southeast side of Chicago to fufill a craving she had for dinner. Tony sauntered past carrying a white plastic bin of dishes from the section of the restaurant used for private parties. His gaze connected with hers and his smile was everything.

She hadn't been attracted to a man since she'd made it back to Chicago so many years ago. And she certainly hadn't dated, though there were a few men who hadn't given up trying. Something about Tony stood out for her. She chalked it up to hormones or something unexplainable. When he walked through that second time, without anything in his arms, she had a full visual of a body that was something the good Lord had made and didn't need to apologize for the perfection. Her mouth went dry and she could barely answer when his deep, resonating voice told her to "Have a great day, ma'am."

Kari wasn't necessarily a "ma'am", but the respectful tone and his gaze were enough to make her answer his smile with one of her own. And that's all it took. She couldn't get him out of her mind for two whole months after she left the restaurant. She finally worked up the nerve to return and inquire about the tall, chocolate green-eyed man who worked there.

"Oh, you mean Toooooony," Stacy, the waitress crooned with a thick Jamaican patois. "Oh, yes. A lotta women like our Tony. He is such a great worker. And not too bad on the eyes, eh?" She slid her order pad toward Kari. "Give me your numba and I'll be sure to give it to him on his next shift."

Kari hesitated a few moments, then scribbled down the digits and her name before returning the pad to Stacy, who gave her a wink, promptly tore the page off then slid it in her front jeans pocket.

Tony didn't call that day, the next day, the next week or even the next few months. Probably wasn't interested in some strange woman who thought she should see what could develop after laying eyes on him just that one time.

Three months later, she had walked into the restaurant to celebrate having made the difficult decision to trade her downtown paralegal job for a freelance paralegal career. Now she would be able to choose what cases she worked on and the lawyers she worked with while she also pursued a law degree.

When Stacy came from the kitchen and saw Kari waiting at the register, her eyes widened to the size of the plate she held in her hand. "Kari. I'm soooooo glad ya came in," she exclaimed. "I lost ya numba when I wash my pants."

Kari's thoughts of the chocolate Adonis had waned over time and so did her disappointment. "I understand all that, but can I get a six piece, some peas and rice, plantain, and—"

"He wants to meet ya." Stacy slid the plate of food she held in front of a burly gentlemen at the bar. "I'll be right back," she said to Kari, and sped away.

Anxiety flowed through Kari. She was mentally unprepared for a meeting with the man she saw that day. And her stomach was protesting about it taking so long to send something on down.

A few moments later, Tony followed a beaming Stacy out of the restaurant's kitchen and towards the dining room, but made a quick stop at the sink to wash his hands. He was even more handsome than she remembered. He eyed Kari with interest, drying a hand on a towel, which he placed on the counter. He searched her eyes for a moment, then extended a hand to Kari and said, "I don't remember the day you came in, but I'll never forget the day you came back."

What a way with words. And that smile. That smile was something that made twinkling stars look tarnished.

"Are you even legal," she asked, grimacing at the fact that she had a few years on him. Only a few.

To that he laughed, which was even better than the smile she had come to love. "I'm twenty-eight."

"And that's supposed to make me feel better?"

"I don't think a number can do that," he countered with a megawatt smile. "And I'd love to call you when I get off work. I'm pulling shifts at two places. So it might be a little late."

"I quit my job today," Kari offered, lowering her gaze to their clasped hands. "Right now I have nothing but time."

"Quit?"

She ignored the curious glances that onlookers sent their way, and focused on him again. "Let's put it this way: I've never been afraid of hard work. But I've grown tired of being expected to pick up the slack for others who won't carry their weight. I swore to myself that any situation that stresses me out or makes me unhappy is not something I need to stick around for."

"Wow," he said, nodding with admiration. "That's something right there."

"But I'm not worried," she explained, wondering why she was rambling like an idiot. "I like eating, driving, and living indoors. So I have a Plan B."

"I appreciate a woman with a plan. She'll always land on her feet." Tony gestured Stacy over from where she and a few other waitresses, cooks and even the owner, were not so discretely listening in, and said, "Put her dinner on my tab. Actually, make it three dinners."

"Are you trying to fatten me up," Kari asked, frowning up at him.

Tony's gaze was intense as he said, "When a woman's trying to work through a plan, the last thing she needs to worry about is where the next few meals are coming from." He pressed a kiss to her upturned palm. "Not a lot of women would choose peace of mind and fairness over a sure paycheck. Do your thing, woman. Do. Your. Thing."

Kari laid her head on Tony's chest, drawing warmth from him. Her life had fast-forwarded to a time where she had so much peace. She had a man who had shown her the kind of love that her father, Daddy, and those clients knew nothing about. Tony called her his *comfort zone*. His *light*. Told her that she was the most beautiful woman in the world— inside and out.

One time, she had asked him why he always said that to her and he replied, "Because the more you hear it, maybe you'll start believing it."

The first lady was a prostitute. Not the kind of woman we want our little girls and young women to emulate.

She closed her eyes against the pain those words had caused her husband, trying to send that warmth to places that had grown cold all over again.

I cut him until I felt better ...

"When it comes to family, I only keep those who want to be kept."
– Jennifer Cole-Addison

Chapter 6

Aridell smiled at Lisa. Somehow, what happened to the woman's bird-brained brother a few minutes before hadn't given her a clue that trying to call Aridell out was not the thing to do.

"Let me tell you something," Aridell began, placing her fists on her hips. "While you're trying to put me on blast about not attending a funeral, I'd like to say thank you for telling me about the funeral *after* it happened."

Lisa's jaw clenched, and color heated her mahogany skin, but she didn't respond.

"In fact, I wouldn't have even known that baby Najee had died, but I just happen to see Tee's post in all caps on my Facebook newsfeed thanking everyone for coming to a funeral that I knew nothing about." Aridell folded her arms across her bosom and chanced a look in Terrance's direction. He quickly hotfooted off to the side, gathering the board and deacons in what looked more like a football huddle. Probably so she couldn't take *him* to task for not telling her about the funeral. She was certain that he had known.

"Nobody tried to hide it from you," Lisa said, lips pursed in a sour line as if she'd tasted something rotten. "So quit lying, talking about you just *happened* to see it."

"Well actually," said a lanky teen pushing a pair of owl-rimmed glasses on his pert nose. "If she wasn't tagged on the post, or if she and Tee didn't interact a lot on Facebook, there's a good chance she *didn't* see it."

All heads turned to the teen.

"See, what comes in a newsfeed is determined by algorithms." The timid nerd glanced at Aridell as if asking for permission to continue.

She gave a small nod. "Yeah, Ricky, tell her about those Ally Rhythms."

"Algorithms," he corrected.

"Yeah. Yeah. What you said."

Ricky turned to Lisa. "If she didn't interact with Tee on Facebook a whole lot, then the only reason Sister Aridell saw the post put up after the funeral is because it came through at a time when a great deal of people were liking it and commenting on it. That's how Facebook works. The more people comment or like a post, the more they interact, the more visible it becomes to other people in their friends list."

"Yeah. What *he* said." Aridell shook her head as she spoke to the people again. "I had to post my condolences on Tee's page. My own niece, and I didn't have a number to call her. Still don't. And you know why that is?"

"Because you thought you were too good for Tee." Lisa cast a wary glance at Tee and a few other family members who had made their way into the aisle, then placed her focus back on Aridell.

"That's the lie she told you," Aridell countered, leaving the spot where she'd stood for the last of the exchange with Terrance. "The real truth is that she cut off all contact with me ten years ago because I wouldn't let her move in with me unless she and her mother signed a living arrangement contract that laid out the rules for Tee living in my house."

There were a few murmurs from the members. And a few nods and shared glances or expressions of admiration.

"A contract?" Lisa snapped, lips curled in disgust. "What's that all about? They're *family*. They didn't have to sign something like that."

"They sure didn't," Aridell shot back. "Just like I didn't have to take responsibility for my out-of-control teenage niece who planned to lay up in my house and do whatever she thought she was grown enough to do," Aridell said putting her gaze on Tee, then to Cathy, her fidgeting mother. "I told her mama to take her little munchkin right back home and deal with her issues herself."

"See, you didn't have to put all that out there," Cathy said, nearly tripping over Sister Karen as she made it to the front of the aisle. "That's private family business."

"You're right, but Lisa made it everyone's business when she put it out there." Aridell took a real good look at the family group near Lisa. "And I find it a little suspect that all of y'all showed up to church today, the very day your brother decided to lose his natural Black mind." Her gaze narrowed at them. "Y'all haven't stepped foot in church since Moses brought down those three tablets."

"It was only two," Tee said with smug smile.

"I know that," Aridell said returning that smile. "He probably threw one away because he knew there was some things even y'all couldn't manage."

The roar of laughter that followed that statement took a few moments to subside.

"This side of the family isn't close for a reason," Aridell confessed. "And it wasn't my doing. Yet, y'all expect me to magically appear at a funeral I wasn't informed about and to support a niece who hasn't said 'come hither' or 'scat kitty' to me since her mother drove off ten years ago. I still love all of you—but from a distance, because when it comes to family, I only keep those who want to be kept."

Lisa's brow furrowed with anger. "I don't have anything to do with the conversation you had with my sister in the past. I just assumed that with you, being the *oldest* aunt on that side of the family, would reach out to your niece during her time of bereavement. For God's sake, the girl lost her four-month-old son." She circled around Aridell as though sizing her up for a boxing match. "It really saddens me to know that you never met your great nephew due to your standoffish ways. You *chose* to be distant from your niece, and I know she tried to contact you."

The congregation's heads were moving between Aridell and the volleys from her family as though watching a tennis match. Some had even lowered in their seats in the same manner most would if watching a live theatre show.

"My number hasn't changed in fifteen years," Aridell countered, hands sliding up over her fleshy hips. "And if I showed you my phone records for all that time, you wouldn't see not a single call from her." Aridell peered at Lisa. "When I finally figured out how to use Facebook, one of the first things I did was send Tee one of those request thingys. But she ignored it. I sent a few more over the years, and she ignored those too." Aridell's gaze left Lisa and landed on Tee, who seemed to wither under that glare. "Then one day out of the blue I got a request *from her*, which I accepted. Not even two seconds later, I got a baby shower invite. No 'how you doing?' No 'how's life been treating you?' Just a request for me to show up with an arm full of presents. Never heard from her again after that. Now you want to call me out about not attending her child's funeral?"

Lisa frowned, seemingly undeterred in her efforts to put Aridell in her place. "The arrangements for baby Najee's home-going services were posted on Facebook for *six whole days*," she said to the nodding agreement of the three Henderson women.

"And I only found out about it last night," Aridell shot back. "Social media is not the place to put important stuff that you want people to know about. Weddings, births, funerals. Those things require a more personal touch. Inbox, text or phone call would have been more appropriate."

"We don't have time for this family drama," Sister Sharon said, getting to her feet.

Her husband pulled the edge of her red blazer and yanked her back to her spot on the pew. He crossed one slack-covered leg over the other and a small smile played about his lips as he put his focus on the center stage of Church Drama 101.

Aridell gestured to a woman a few pews away. "Pass me that iPad thing, Terry."

The woman rummaged through Aridell's purse, procured the tablet and brought it over. A few clicks on the messenger app and Aridell had pulled up the visual of the only message exchange with the niece in question. "You see that? An in-box to Tee from two years ago. I gave her my phone number and let her know, several times, that I'd like to keep in touch. She didn't."

Lisa took the tablet and scrolled through the message.

"I might not be all that technical, but I am smarter than the average bear, Boo-Boo," Aridell said as she extracted the tablet from Lisa's hand and passed it back to Terry. "And I can realize when someone doesn't want a connection with me. Tee's mad at her daddy for not being in her life, and I can understand that. And she's mad at me because I wasn't going to let her run over me like she was doing to her mama back then."

Lisa shifted her stance, angling so that her niece could see her clearly as she said to Aridell, "I have my own personal views about churchified folks like you who love outsiders more than their own flesh and blood." She shrugged as though none of this conversation was of any consequence—or that she'd started this whole mess.

Aridell waited for the murmurs echoing in the church to subside before she said, "I understand that you're all in your feelings right now. I get that. I mean, you're her maternal aunt and the loss of the baby is so fresh. But you need to recognize that calling me out—here—because you feel some kind of way, is not the thing to do."

Lisa glanced at the congregation and squared her shoulders. "I pray that one day in the near future, the animosity or obstacles blocking this family from communicating will be resolved."

"I'm all for it whenever they are," Aridell said with a sweeping gesture that encompassed Lisa, Tee, Cathy, and their other family members. She sighed, weary of the entire exchange and ready to get on with the real business at hand. "But what you did today wasn't a step in that direction. And why didn't you call me yourself? You have my number even if Tee doesn't. You know where I am every Wednesday, Friday, and Sunday, even if she doesn't."

Lisa waved her off with a striped manicured hand. "Puh-lease. I know I speak for the whole family when I say it's pitiful and beneath you to blame us for you alienating yourself."

Aridell reached out a hand. "My cell, please."

Terry complied and Aridell flipped through the contacts. She selected one, touched the screen to connect the call.

The phone rang and vibrated in Lisa's purse on the pew.

"Go on," Aridell suggested. "Pick it up."

Lisa gave a wary glance at her purse as Tee maneuvered around Aridell, fished the phone out and turned the screen to face her family. It showed Aridell's name and phone number clearly.

Lisa snatched the phone and over the sounds of everyone's "ooohs and aaaah's she ground out, "It's over now. My great nephew's dead and buried. Your response to this conversation was just what I expected."

"Are we done yet?" Aridell asked, as murmurs from the congregation echoed around them as though they were also tired of all this drama in one Sunday morning service. "Either y'all are gonna work toward bridging the gap between our families, or you're gonna stand here for the next ten hours hurling accusations. Either way, I don't have the time." Aridell stood, and walked in the direction of the door. "Your brother stirred an ugly pot and I have every intention of turning off the fire and taking him off the stove."

Chapter 7

"You've always been so guarded," Tony said in a low tone. "So I didn't push. Not even after we got married. But ..." He looked deeply into her eyes, adjusting his position next to her on the sofa. "I love you. Nothing will ever change that. Not the past. Not the present. Not the future."

This wonderful man had loved her from day one. Had promised that no harm would come to her. And he had kept his word on that, and so many other things.

She scanned the living room, taking in the abstract artwork that was a perfect complement to each piece of modern styled furniture. All part of the memories that she was afraid she would taint when she shared her story.

Tony pulled her close and stroked a hand across her back. "It's something to know that my woman's pain runs so deep that she won't share it, even with me."

"You knew?" she asked, pulling away so she could look up at him.

"I've counseled too many woman and girls from the church to not know."

She let that walk through her mind for a moment before saying, "I never told you because that part of my life isn't something I want to remember."

Tony was silent for a few ticks of time before saying, "I understand."

Kari left his hold, putting a few inches of space between them. "I'll just gather up my things and—"

"You're not going anywhere," he said, closing the distance to reclaim her into an embrace. "If I let you walk out that door because of some self-righteous, ambitious—"

"I never wanted to interfere with your calling," she said, trying to steel herself against the pain that filled her. "You said you made a promise to the Almighty when he spared your life, that from that point on you'd do His work. You can't do God's work if you don't have a church. If I leave, then you can get your church back."

"They can have that," he said in a tone so soft but certain, she couldn't find a way to answer. "Evidently, all this time I've been teaching and they haven't been listening. Church is not about a building. It's supposed to be about healing people and giving them the tools to heal themselves." He cupped her face in his hands. "Either I fooled myself or the entire congregation was doing nothing more than giving lip service."

Kari stared up at him, wondering how God could allow something that happened in her life to disrupt His plans for a man who'd been the greatest example of someone who lived with integrity, compassion, and determination.

"I serve God through serving people who need it most." He pressed a kiss to her forehead. "And I want my wife to be very much a part of that."

"This could happen again," she admitted, trying to keep her voice level. "New place, new people, and it could happen all over again."

"And it won't matter," he countered. "So many women have a past like yours. The problem is that when people try to hide their skeletons, there's always some hound dog who'll sniff them out and dig up the bones."

Kari frowned as she said, "I don't understand your logic."

"Remember when it was all in the news that Janet Jackson's husband was demanding a ridiculous amount of money from their divorce, even though they had a pre-nup? He was threatening to go public about some things if she didn't pay up."

"Yes, so?"

Tony stroked a hand through her hair. "If she had told her own secrets, she wouldn't have been in a position where he could hold her financially hostage."

Now *that* got her attention.

"And I don't want you held emotionally hostage by people like Terrance Henderson," he said. "If you don't believe anything else, please believe me when I say that what happened today hasn't interfered with anything concerning me and you," Tony said. "I took vows with you before God and that right there comes before anything else."

"You'd really leave the church for me?"

"I'll always be a minister, sweetheart," he said, giving her a smile that touched her heart. "But my service to God isn't tied to a building. It's tied to my relationship with Him and with you."

Kari looked up at him, unable to voice anything around the emotion that swelled in her heart.

"We're going to work on us so that we're solid and our relationship is tight. And we'll start with you answering a question that only you can answer."

She stiffened.

Tony scrunched his eyebrows together, expression filled with concern. "Noooo, I'm not asking about your past." He stroked a hand across her face. "If you're not ready to share your truth, that's your right. For now, I just want you to tell me how you think we can be of service to God."

"You're asking *me*?" she asked in a breathy whisper, placing a hand over her heart. "Seriously?"

"Why not?" he asked, laughing at her incredulous expression. "You're the woman God sent me. I want to hear what you have to say."

She extracted herself from his hold, giving his question some thought. "You know what I admired about Jesus?"

Tony tilted his head, waiting.

"He never hung out with the people in the church," she said. "In fact, He wasn't real fond of them."

"Right about now, I understand His point," Tony said in a dry tone. "This church has been more a test of my faith than anything else."

She tried not to smile, moved to him, and entered his embrace once again. "He came to heal the broken-hearted. That's what the good book says. And to me, there's no one more broken than the woman I was before."

What she didn't say out loud was … *The broken woman I still am today.*

Chapter 8

"We need to get some dinner," Kari said, sighing the moment her stomach gave a growling reminder that she hadn't eaten anything since early that morning.

Tony held her firmly in his embrace. "Can we eat after we talk?"

"That smothered chicken has been calling my name since Sunday School. We can talk all you want, but I need to put some soul food strength in me."

He laughed, snaked his arm around Kari's waist and led her into their navy and white gourmet kitchen that he insisted she have so she could continue to perfect those already stellar cooking skills. Side-by-side, they heated up the food and prepared two plates that they placed outside on the solarium's patio table rather than in the dining room where they normally shared their meals every night.

For a while they ate in silence, each seemingly lost in their own thoughts—most of which were about the person sitting across the table.

"All right," Kari said after she'd made a little headway into their meal of smothered chicken, rice and gravy, green beans, candied yams and cornbread. "I know you've been holding back what you really want to say, so let's have at it."

Tony studied her as he finished off a mouthful of food. "I'm disappointed that I haven't been the kind of man that you felt you could trust with your past," he said, placing his fork on the edge of his plate.

She parted her lips to protest, but he held up his hand to stave it off.

"People have opened up to me with the darkest parts of their lives, but yet my own wife wasn't able to." He trained those dark brown orbs on her, his bottom lip held prisoner for a few seconds before he released it. "What does that say about me?"

The anguish in his voice, the glassy shine of pain in his eyes, almost felled her completely. She reached out for him and he hesitated a slight moment before taking her hands in his.

"It had nothing to do with you," she confessed, suddenly losing what was left of her appetite. Her secrets had created a chasm in their marriage she never intended. "I mean, how exactly does a woman tell the man she loves, 'By the way, I used to whore for a living'?"

"For starters, she wouldn't put it quite that bluntly."

"But it's the truth," she countered, and for a moment she was back in that police interview room with that blonde officer who wanted Kari to alter the story so she wouldn't serve a single day behind bars. "That's exactly the truth."

"You were … fourteen?" he said, pushing his plate toward the center of the table. "Fourteen-year-olds don't enter that life without some help. Evidently, you were abused by someone who made their living off setting young girls up as prey."

Kari closed her eyes as his summary hit all the way home.

"When you were in high school, is that something you set out to do?"

"No, I … I mean, when I was a girl," she replied. "I didn't know what I wanted to be in life, but it wasn't *that*."

Tony brought the tips of her fingers to his lips, the tingle of warmth whipped through her. He always managed to do that so well.

Kari looked away, unable to make eye contact while sharing the details of a world he couldn't begin to understand. After taking a few deep breaths, releasing them slowly, Kari began to unearth some of what she'd buried so deep.

"There was this guy who worked in the cafeteria of my high school." She shook her head; still unable to believe she'd been so naïve back then. "I thought he loved me, but what he loved was that I was young and dumb. We all were," she admitted. "He was playing three of us, but he chose me to be his girlfriend. I felt so special," she said dryly. "This cute older guy was buying me things, sneaking me out of school, taking me places." Kari left the table and looked out on the Koi pond at the center of the lush garden she'd taken three years to get picture perfect— the pinks, purples, and whites and an arraying shades of green made it the most relaxing place to be. Tony was by her side in an instant.

"I ran away from home and ended up riding with him to Memphis to meet his family," she whispered. "His "family" turned out to be those two classmates of mine and another group of girls not much older than I was. We had to call him Daddy. The first night, Trina tried to escape. He beat her so bad she couldn't open her eyes for a whole week."

Kari left the glass-encased solarium and went further out on the patio, stepped forward onto the grass, letting the softness tickle her bare feet. "Not a day went by that he didn't rape at least one of us. He made the rest of us watch." She looked over her shoulder at Tony, who kept his expression neutral, but she saw the vein throbbing at his temple. "He had high-end customers that wanted fresh, young meat."

Tony came to her, pulled her against him. She welcomed the warmth because a chill had settled inside her despite the sun's rays shining down on them. What a beautiful day to share such an ugly story. It almost seemed surreal.

"I made it through my first rape the night I arrived. It was … brutal," she said as her voice cracked on that last word. "But I became used to living with pain. It prepared me to survive everything else."

And that "everything else" was no small thing.

Tony listened without judgment, soothed her when she needed it most. Allowed her space when the anger resurfaced and she couldn't contain any part of it. The sobs, the tears, the anger at God for letting it happen—Tony absorbed it all and gave her so much of himself. His love was giving her a healing that trying to erase the past from her memory had never accomplished.

"I was a church girl growing up," she said after finishing a condensed version of her story. She gripped those muscular arms of his, gathering strength from his touch. "That's all I ever did—church, school, and home. My parents wouldn't let me watch television unless it was the Christian station. I had to read the Bible, chapters at a time. I couldn't wear pants, makeup, jewelry—none of that." She closed her eyes, allowing the image of her parents to surface. They, too, were part of the memories she had buried deep. They would never forgive her for what happened. Would never accept a daughter who had become tainted with the filth Daddy forced her to wallow in.

"All I knew was those three things, so I never imagined the kinds of people that were out there. My parents never warned me about that. And Daddy would do—correction, Daddy would make *us* do—whatever it took to keep the money rolling in. If a man liked girls who were comatose, Daddy would give one of the girls drugs that paralyzed her but still kept her conscious enough to see, hear and feel everything that was being done to her. Some of those girls hadn't even experienced their first cycle yet. And they received the same horrible education that I did."

Kari shivered as the rest of the memories tumbled forward, begging to be released. "And then they went to a whole different level."

Tony held out his hand and she inched hers inside his. He tightened his grip as though sending her a silent dose of courage. Lord knows she needed it.

"Daddy was about to take a few of us down to Mexico to film some type of movie that included … horses." She paused long enough to let the sordid meaning behind that sink in. "That was a new thing. We stopped being shocked a long time before then."

She glanced up at Tony, saw his jaw working as though biting back his anger, and wondered if she should have shared that information. He wanted to know all of it, but could he handle it? He was ready to kill

Terrance Henderson for calling her a whore. How much anger would surface if he knew how much of a whore she had been?

"All I could think about was that my mama didn't know where I was," she whispered, letting her feet graze the waters of the pond. "And if she knew what I was doing, she'd know just how worthless I was."

"Your mother would never think that," Tony said, and she wanted to laugh at the certainty in his voice. But she knew better.

"She shunned every family member who wasn't a church-going Christian. She stopped speaking to my Uncle Victor and anyone who accepted him, all because he was gay. My cousin Shante started singing secular music and my mother wouldn't allow me anywhere near that girl." Kari's gaze connected with Tony's. "So don't tell me she wouldn't turn her back on someone like me. I've seen her do it to too many people. Even the ones in church."

Tony's lips set in a thin resigned line, and she waited for his response. "Maybe she's grown since then. At some point, you have to give her a chance."

"She was right, Tony. If I hadn't—"

"No!"

The word was said so vehemently that she took a step back.

"You're not going there with that whole 'if I hadn't thing," he said, and his tone brooked no resistance. "This isn't about self-guilt. I want to know what happened because I need to know how to help my wife. I can't give any more energy to anyone else until I make sure *you're* straight. That *we're* straight. And if that means me not having another church for a while, so be it." Tony pressed a kiss to her temple. "My wife comes first. I made a commitment to God, which I will fulfill. But I made a vow to you and He needs me to be about that business right about now."

Kari stiffened, trying to hold in the emotions that his words brought on. She cried into the wall of his chest for the longest time, tried to get her voice working again to finish at least some of the story.

"I tried to get away," she said after several moments had passed. "Even made it as far as the bus station one time, but I didn't know

Daddy had his people there. People he paid to inform him when young girls got off the bus alone or if one of his girls tried to leave the city. They all knew who we were. Even the police. We serviced them sometimes, too." She stilled at the memory of the one officer she had worked up the courage to ask for help. He had done the exact opposite. Daddy had served her up to him for an entire week to teach her a valuable lesson— there was no help for her anywhere.

"He'd go back to Chicago from time to time and bring in more girls. I saw more classmates down there in Memphis than I ever did in class." She wrapped her arms about Tony's waist and laid her head on his broad chest. His heart rate was a lot faster than it should have been. Seems that he was doing all he could not to let rage set in. Her hero. Her husband. Her love.

"I tried to get a client to help me—told him to just take me with him and I'd make it from there. The man promised he would. Then after he was done using me, he told Daddy what I said."

"That night, Daddy nearly beat me to death, then he brought in this six-year-old girl, crying, screaming for her mother. She ran to each of the girls in the apartment, begging, pleading with them to help her." Her voice hitched and for a moment she was unable to speak.

"It's all right," Tony said, stroking a comforting hand over the lower part of her back.

The memory of the way Daddy gazed at that child ran Kari's blood cold all over again. "They were so cruel," she finally managed to say. "They were taunting her, telling her what Daddy was going to do to her. She was screaming, crying ..." Kari closed her eyes, trying to block out the image of that pretty little girl. "Then she ran to me. Her voice was so raw from crying that she couldn't get any more words out. My own eyes were just as wet and puffy as hers. She had no way of knowing I'd just been beaten. She could have thought in her little mind that I was shedding tears for her. Whatever it was, she latched onto me and wouldn't let go." Kari found it hard to swallow. "She was so tiny. Only a ... little girl."

She removed herself from Tony's hold, wrapped her arms about her own midriff, but the action provided no comfort. "For years, he made me do anything and everything. And he was going to put her through that?"

Kari shook her head and Tony came to her, pulled her back into the safety of his arms. "She needed me and I guess I needed her too. I couldn't let it happen again."

She looked up at her husband, those green eyes sparkling with anger that he barely was able to keep under control.

"So later that night, I used a kitchen knife," she said. "The only sharp one we had. We'd been so afraid of him that not a single one of us had the courage to do anything. And trust me, we had plenty of opportunities. But he'd pit us against each other. You couldn't do anything without one of the others running to tell him about it. He encouraged that by rewarding those who told." Kari's mind flickered to Tangie and Martina—the main ones. "Sometimes they'd get fewer clients to service the next day or maybe he'd take them out for dinner or a movie to thank them for looking out for him."

Tony's eyebrows drew in. "How did you manage to get past the others without someone noticing the knife in your hand?"

"Like I said, she wouldn't leave my side," Kari answered, tamping down her emotions or she wouldn't be able to finish. "Clung to me as tightly as the cheap clothes Daddy gave me to wear. So when I went into the kitchen and slid the knife from the drawer, her body hid what I was doing." Kari dropped her head and let her arms fall to her side. "To this day, I don't know whether he bruised or broke my ribs in that beating. One good thing that came out of it was that I couldn't be set up with any clients for a few days. But I knew he would come to me that night because any girl who wasn't out making him money had another job to do—keeping him happy."

Kari looked out at the Koi swimming about each other. The place was peaceful and one of her greatest escapes—besides the arms of her husband.

"When he called for me to come to his bedroom, the little girl wouldn't let me go without her," she said. "I whispered to her that everything was going to be fine and that she should wait outside the door. Daddy said, 'I might've wanted the new piece to join in, but I see you want me all to yourself.'"

She didn't. And then again, she did.

"You don't have to tell the rest if it's too much for you," Tony said, pushing a wayward strand of her hair away from her face.

"I need to tell it, to take away its power to haunt me," she said, but still couldn't make eye contact with him. "He was sitting on the edge of the bed and gestured for me to get on my knees in front of him. He unzipped his pants, leaned back and closed his eyes. He never saw the knife because it was in my waistband and covered by my top. I slid it out and sliced him across his genitals."

Daddy's sharp intake of breath had been a welcome sound. But it was the little girl's scream and the fear of what would happen if Daddy got off that bed that spurred Kari into action. He wouldn't wait to send her to the slicer. He would do the work himself.

"I aimed for his knees the second time," she said. "To make sure he couldn't walk out of the room. Then his arms. And I kept going until his screams brought the others running."

All of them—his bottom girl, the new girls, the ones who'd lasted a while, the ones he said had lived past their usefulness—congregated at the door, peering in at her handiwork.

"I cut him so many times that I lost count," Kari admitted. "His bottom girl yelled for the others to pull me off of him. No one made a move, and I kept cutting him. Tangie was the one who dragged me off the bed."

Kari locked gazes with Tony. "She might've saved his life, because I would've kept going until there was nothing left."

"If all you have to offer me are the crumbs of your life, don't be upset when I show you that I'm just not that hungry." -- Naleighna Kai

Chapter 9

"You were wrong as two left feet," Aridell said, shaking her fist at Henderson and his cronies. "There's a proper way to do things, and this wasn't it." She gave a sideways glance at Lisa. "Must run in the family."

"I have every right," he shot back. "This church has been in *our* family for nearly one hundred years."

"And it would have been back in the family in a manner of time," she countered, seething at his senselessness. "You needed to work under Pastor Kimbrough, learn how he does things. *Then* you'd be able to run a church. You don't blindside a man and try to jack him for his congregation just 'cause you don't want to wait your turn," she roared. "The man built this congregation from a storefront to a building of our own. You and your cronies waited for him to do all the hard work. And now you want to step your tired behind in and take over? That's not how it's done."

Applause rippled through the congregation and Henderson scanned the parishioners for some sign of support. He had lost a few more.

"Every last one of you," she said, waggling a finger at the board and deacons. "Mark my words. When things aren't done in God's timing, it's not gonna work." She turned, angling so she could glare at her nephew. "Be honest, you're not trying to lead these folks because you've been called. You want to be the pastor because the money the church is bringing in is calling you. Well, I don't have time for your madness." She faced the board and deacons, raising a brow at their grim expressions. "I'm going to pastor's house to make this right."

Henderson glanced at the board members and then back to Aridell. "I don't care what they said," he shot back, gesturing toward the choir members and the Faithful Few. "He can't come back here. Him or his who—wife. His wife."

"If I was him, I wouldn't want to," Aridell quipped with a hand on her fleshy hip. "Ain't nothing but heathens trying to run this camp."

Murmurs and quiet conversations followed that statement.

"You want to judge that woman like you got a right. Like what she did in the past makes a matter on who she is today." Aridell swept a stony gaze at Henderson's supporters.

He swaggered forward, lowering his head to look at her. "You're telling me that you're going to side against family that's been in this church all these years?"

"I'm not siding against anybody," she said. "I'm on the side of what's right. Same way those twelve should be. Y'all didn't do right by that woman, letting this knucklehead spill that filth and call her out of her name. That wasn't right. And that's something you're gonna answer for." She put her focus on a scowling Henderson. "I really want to club you upside the head with Vera's cane."

Henderson didn't have a comeback for that. Vera extended said cane just in case. Aridell shook her head so she'd put it away. She did so, begrudgingly, but gave Henderson the "evil eye" for good measure.

Aridell noticed that the choir members were trying to adjust their robes. "Go on, take them off," she commanded and they quickly complied. "We obviously ain't having morning service around here today." Some murmured their thanks and others shot her grateful glances.

"Wasn't it Bertice Berry that said, 'There's two kinds of people. Ones that show up before the party to help out and the ones that show up after all the work's been done. Never confuse the two'?" Aridell leaned in, pushed an index finger in Henderson's chest. "I know exactly who you are. And just because the Bible says we're sheep, that doesn't mean we can't recognize when the wolf walks in." She sized him up with her eyes, then peered around him to the men moving in to flank him. "Listening to this fool whisper sweet nothings in your ear. Well, he ain't sweet and he ain't been about nothing." She lifted her hand in their direction. "Y'all just scared and trying to bring a minister in here that's not gonna make y'all do some real work. Pastor Kimbrough wants us to get out in this community and do something to make a difference, not just come up in here every Sunday bragging about how holy we are."

Brother Matthew broke away from the others to say, "We're not equipped to go out there and deal with them thugs and drug dealers and pimps."

Aridell held out a hand for her purse, which Sister Terry passed to Sister Vera, who promptly supplied it to Aridell. She rifled through the contents and pulled out her trusty gun. "I am."

Several gasps echoed off the walls.

"The Qur'an says 'Trust in the Lord, but tie your camel." She slid the weapon back into her purse.

"We're not Muslim," Brother Matthew growled, wisely putting some space between them.

"And we're not stupid either," Aridell shot back, grinning at the fact that he was trembling a little. "The Bible tells us to put on the whole armor of God. Well sometimes you have to have the kind of armor that people understand." She patted her purse. "And this right here starts a conversation or ends one. Now let's be about business instead of hiding behind this here brick wall, while the police and those thugs go on killing our people with surprising regularity. Innocent kids are getting gunned down every day. People sitting in their homes and minding their business get shot by stray bullets." She shook her head. "Chicago's the deadliest city because we're not out there trying to make it the Godliest one."

A few "Amens" and "That's rights" followed those words.

"Pastor Kimbrough wants us to do what we can to change all that," she said, sauntering up the aisle. "And I'm with him. Y'all can sit here and go down in flames if you want to. But I'm going to be out in those streets where the real ministry's happening."

"So now you're a community leader," Henderson taunted, to the laughs of the men nearest him.

"Better than being a bottom feeder." She gave him a pat on the cheek and walked toward the Faithful Few, who followed her out the door along with Vera, Ricky, and nearly all of choir members and the musicians.

Chapter 10

"Going through all that made me sure that God would never be able to love me anymore," Kari said, tempering her emotions. "You have to remember that I grew up with a mama who was always talking about sin and shame, fire and brimstone. Our preacher said over and over again that the Bible says we're just dirty dishrags in God's sight."

Tony held a hand up, halting her next words as he said, "See, that's why it's so important for people to read the Bible for themselves. It says that our *righteousness* is as filthy rags, not that *we* are like dirty dishrags. Simply put, that scripture revolves around the fact that God isn't pleased by, or impressed with, our self-righteousness because we can never do enough good to blot out our sinful nature. Only God's own righteousness can cleanse us."

"Well the *God* they introduced me to was just waiting for us to mess up so we could be punished. There was no mention of a God of grace and mercy that I hear you teach about." She sighed, and Tony touched a hand to her face to bring her a sense of calm. Then he led her to the swing and settled her beside him.

"When I ran away and found myself being sold to men, raped and beaten, I could just picture this mean old God looking down from

Heaven and saying, "You deserved everything you got."

"No," Tony said, shaking her a little. That's not the kind of God we believe in." His green eyes softened, glossy with unshed tears.

"I saw and experienced things that no one, especially a child, should ever have to," she confessed. "And I wondered how God could turn a blind eye to that and all the other hurt and pain in the world. I was so mad at Him. So very mad." Kari tensed in his arms, because truthfully she was *still* angry with God. "It was a blonde policewoman who saved what little life I had. She called in a lawyer who worked a deal so that I wouldn't serve a day behind bars if I testified against Daddy. It didn't come to that. They used me to force Daddy to make a deal and give up the names of his contacts and clients to save himself from a lifetime behind bars. And when the trial was over, and they'd brought several of those men to court, do you know what that woman did?"

She took her husband's hand, opened it up, placed an imaginary object on his palm, and closed his fingers over it. "She put fifty folded twenty-dollar bills in my hand. Bus fare back to Chicago, enough for food and to keep me going for a while." Kari felt a small smile flicker across her face. "She said that since the day she took the knife out of my hand, she'd been praying that I would find God and get a chance at a full and satisfying life. But I stopped trying to find God a long time ago," she admitted. "I didn't want that God I grew up with."

"But God was with you. Believe me." Tony traced a finger across her jawbone. "He turned your life around the same way he did mine. And look at what you did with your second chance. Got your GED, went to community college then a university, got your bachelor's—"

"Then fell in love with a man who wanted to be a minister of all things." Kari laughed, but there was no joy in it. "Me, who still had serious doubts about God." She gave him a sideways glance.

"That's why you kept trying to break up with me?" He clamped his mouth shut and he shook his head as those green eyes lit with understanding.

"I was afraid," she said, looking away from him. "How could I love and support a man who believed so much in something I didn't believe in myself? That was wrong on so many levels." She bit her bottom lip, thinking back to many years ago. "When you received that offer from the church to become the pastor, I tried to leave again. You deserved a better future wife than me. But you wouldn't let me go."

"Not then," he said, tightening his hold on her. "And certainly not now. People are going to come at me every which way but loose, and I want to handle it with my woman by my side."

Kari didn't have the words to respond to him. Tony was so steadfast in two things—his love for God, and his love for her.

"The way you love me is beginning to help me understand how God could love me," she whispered, and closed her eyes to still the emotions warring within. "I wasn't there to witness the miracles of Christ in the Bible. But I am here to witness how you love me. And that, to me, is a miracle. It seems like God used you so He could reach me."

She angled her feet and pushed off, giving the swing a slow rhythm. Kari laid her head on his chest, as his arms wound about her shoulders. "I started watching you, listening to you; learning from you. And for me, you became an example of what God's love could be like. I mean, you said you weren't striving for perfection, only to feel complete. And you know what? Completion is as real as it could get for me too."

Tony's hand lowered until it landed about her waist. "I'm glad something I've done brought you closer to God," he said with a brightness in his eyes that faded as he dryly added, "I only wish I could have done the same for my congregation."

"You didn't fail, Tony," she said, placing a hand on his massive chest. "Those members who sided with Henderson, they're just human."

"But they're supposed to be striving to be non-judgmental; not to be … *that* way. They were so quick to believe him; so quick to judge you. Without any proof other than his word."

There was a lot of truth in that. "I never trusted him," she confessed, laying her head on his shoulder. "But the board wanted someone with the family name."

"Well, they have him, all right," he said with a nod. "But a lot of good that's going to do."

"What are you saying?"

"That you and I are going to do what I've been talking about for the past year. Chicago is at a boiling point. We're taking God to the streets."

Kari's heart filled with so much pride. Her husband was consistent if nothing else. She liked the idea of starting something of their own instead of trying to fit a square peg of dreams into a round hole of outright opposition.

"Earlier, you asked me what kind of ministry we should be in. I think it should be one that helps women and children who've been victims of sexual abuse and sex trafficking."

"I can get with that," he said, brow furrowed in thought. "But that can happen a little later. We need to focus on us right now. Get our thing tight. So that no one can came at us again the way Henderson did."

Buoyed by a sense of hope, she slid off the swing, extended her hand and led him inside.

Kari wrapped her arms around her husband, deepening the kiss they shared, feeling the same heat she'd felt the first night they made love. A kind of heat and passion she'd never thought she would feel. She felt it with him, only him, and loved him for the gentleness and care he had taken with her from day one.

The first time Tony came over to her apartment in Mermaid Towers of South Shore, she had breakfast waiting for him, even though it was close to midnight. He said breakfast was his favorite meal—homemade biscuits, cheese grits, eggs, and bacon—simple things. Between his two jobs, there was only this short window of time where they could be face to face.

He'd eaten every bite as they chatted about his work and a little about her Plan B of becoming a freelance paralegal while she pursued her goal of gettin a law degree. She had taken that money Nancy had given her and the rest that her lawyer sent from the FBI as "resettlement" funds since she refused to enter into their witness protection program. Both were used in a systematic approach to making it go as far as possible.

After Tony polished off the last of the cheese grits, he was silent a moment. A small sense of alarm went through her.

"Do you have a computer?" he asked, his tone as solemn as his expression.

"Sure," she said, frowning at how his shoulders squared as if bracing for something.

"You mind if I pull up some info?"

Kari left the dining room table, led him past her bedroom and into the small space she'd converted into an office. He slid into her executive chair and tapped into the Internet. Soon he was in the Cook County Criminal Division website. Seconds after that, he typed in his full name, date of birth and pulled up a page that had more information than she'd ever thought to ask.

Tony angled the screen so she could read it fully. He remained silent as she took in how much of a bad boy he'd been. Possession of a weapon. Possession of a controlled substance. He'd been a guest of Cook County jail. It wasn't a long rap sheet, but not necessarily the kind of thing a woman was looking for in a mate, either.

All she had known was that he'd been trying to live his life on the right edge, working at the restaurant during the day and pulling the evening shift in the document services department of an advertising agency. She scanned the screen again, and for a moment, newspaper reports of women who had unwittingly invited a monster into their lives flitted through her mind.

Truthfully, if he'd wanted to hurt her, he'd already had ample opportunity. And she didn't get that vibe from him. But she'd been wrong about Daddy. At least this one was honest about his sins up front.

She glanced at him, and raised a questioning brow. Then, like a shot in the arm, a thought entered her mind. Kari put her focus back on the screen and searched for the one thing that was an instant deal breaker— domestic violence. Sexual assault. There could be a lot of things that hadn't made it into print, so she glanced at him again, and voiced the one question that could also end things before it started ...

"Have you ever ... hurt a woman? Raped her?"

Chapter 11

"Never," he said, and the intensity behind that one word made her breathe a sigh of relief.

"How long were you in?"

"Small stretch. Three years," he replied. "Drugs and a weapon meant I could've been in there until all three of my sisters became great grandparents." Tony stood, moved to the opposite side of the room and looked out on that small sliver of Lake Michigan the window offered. "Met a man inside who'd given his life to God. Saw how much respect he got from everyone. He wasn't afraid of anything. Not the guards, not the gangs, not the Aryans. That impressed me." Tony leaned his shoulder against the wall, still keeping his focus outside. "We talked a lot, especially about questions I've always had about God and religion. His simple take on the most complex things made God real to me."

Tony left the window and came to stand in front of her, but he didn't make any attempt to touch her.

"I made a promise to myself while I was in there that when I got out I'd get into the seminary and study the Bible for myself; that I'd

be about the business of making sure no one else in my family started slinging dope or getting into the same situation I did because they feel there's no other choice."

Kari left the computer, brushed past him and went into the living room. A handsome, hardworking man who was intelligent and ambitious had landed in her lap. He had some serious baggage, but he was up front about it. It wasn't like there were a lot of heterosexual men on this side of the bars who weren't married, or players, or didn't have a sordid history that made them off-limits to women.

When Tony came into the room, she locked a dark brown gaze with his green one and said, "I won't hold your past against you, if you don't hold my past against me."

He let out a long slow breath, pulled her into an embrace that seemed to go on forever. For the first time, she felt something that had eluded her for so long. She felt safe.

Kari stayed in his arms that night. The chemistry between them was so strong but no matter how much she pressed against him, gave the physical signs that she wanted more, Tony didn't take the bait. Before she slipped into sleep within the comfort of his arms, he whispered, "I'm going to marry you."

There was a certainty in his voice that made her look over her shoulder at him.

"You don't even know me," she replied, wondering if something about her made him think she was an easy mark for that kind of empty-promise. But over those few months of conversation, she'd come to know him enough that if he said something, he would work like crazy to make it happen.

"I know enough," he said placing a kiss on the crown of her head. "A woman going hard at her Plan B and making it work is a woman I want on my team. Always."

Tony kissed her lips then and she so wanted him to make love to her, but he wouldn't take things there. "I made a promise to myself," he said. "That we wouldn't make love until you gave me the privilege and pleasure of making you my wife. And I'm going to keep that. No matter how much I want you. I want you to always feel you can trust me. That my word is my bond."

The words were like a balm to her soul. Trust. Openness. Integrity.

Six months later, from the Honeymoon Suite of the Drake Hotel, Mrs. Kari Kimbrough admired the beautiful princess-cut floating halo diamond he had slipped on her finger earlier that day. She pressed a kiss to her husband's lips while he removed the wedding dress, unveiling her a little at a time before placing it on the nearest chair. She arched her body toward him and his mouth descended on hers, tasting her, teasing her. Her white silk and lace corset joined the gown and soon his tux and the rest of his clothing was in the mix.

Tony stood behind her, lips placed on the small curve of her bare shoulder. Soft kisses on the base of her neck sent feather-soft shocks of pleasure through her body. He pulled her to him, connected them so close she could feel how aroused he'd become. His hands spread out, stroking down the front of her body and grazing her breasts ever so gently before splaying on her abdomen, bracing her against him. A woodsy fragrance mingled with his own earthy scent made her inhale him; made her want to taste the sweet saltiness of his skin.

"Are you ready for me?" he asked.

Those wonderful hands of his lowered, stroking the lace material covering her heated core, a rhythmic blend of exploration and queries.

"Are you ready for me?"

She was too overwhelmed with the pleasant sensations to put voice to the one word in her mind.

He asked yet again and she finally managed a breathy, "Yes."

Tony took his time exploring the silky softness of her hair. Kari's breathing hitched and she found it so hard to take a solid breath. His movements, slow, deliberate, gentle were her absolute undoing. It had never been this beautiful

Tony touched her, teased her, pleased her to the point that she trembled in a way that her body had never done. She was used to pain. That's all sex had ever been. Fear and pain. But this, this right here ...

This man was making sure she never wanted for anything less than for a man to worship her body just like this.

Sensations were like a river running through her soul. He pressed a kiss to the base of her neck, traipsed those lips to a point that she angled her head so her lips could join his.

Then he was with her, his body streamlined against hers in a way that allowed their breaths to mingle; and she opened to him, inviting him in for a lengthy visit. Tony showed her what love felt like, what it tastes like. Showed her how the world could end on a scream of passion and be reborn with a sigh of pleasure.

True to his word, Tony had made the first strides to get into Chicago Theological Seminary. Because of his criminal background, he wasn't eligible to receive grants, loans or financial aid. He'd worked two jobs to put himself through school, refusing to accept a dime of Kari's money. And she had offered so many times. Especially since her freelance paralegal business was thriving even more than she imagined and she'd added four more staff to fulfill a contract with a civil case involving the oil spill in the gulf.

"I don't ever want it said that I'm only with you because I needed a ride," he'd said, and his tone spoke to the fact that he would not broach the subject again. "I'm going to make it happen. Trust me. Might take a little longer, but I'll get there." He'd pulled her to him, stroked an index finger down her cheeks. "You just keep loving me and encouraging me. Oh, and keep those good meals coming."

Tony had a knack for washing away any worries. And he also had a head for business.

He started a unique business of procuring artwork and written works by inmates, and selling them to support their families and put money on their books. It brought him in a substantial income allowing him to use the profits to open an individual stock trading account. Then he worked up enough cash and established an account as a corporate entity to trade on a higher level. Then he opened a gallery and bookstore that displayed the works and continued his efforts to help ex-cons who were trying to get their lives together. His gallery now had five locations—Detroit,

Milwaukee, Chicago, Atlanta and New York. Most of them managed by the son of the man who he'd met in prison who had changed his life.

With so many doors closed to men with his kind of past, he forged an avenue that brought in an income that took care of Kari and amply took care of their needs while allowing him to focus on his studies and graduate from the seminary.

She had kept her end of the bargain, and Anthony J. Kimbrough had more than kept his.

The one thing he had never pressed her about was those "missing" years of her life. Now it seemed that they were the very things that could cost him everything he'd worked so hard to build.

She had told him, "I won't hold your past against you, if you won't hold my past against me."

Never imagining that years later she'd managed to keep that past from him; or that fate would force her to confront it in such an ugly way.

Chapter 12

Kari and Tony were so deep into their kiss that what happened at church earlier and the outside world as a whole, ceased to exist. They made it to the master bedroom, ready to join in that all too familiar dance, when …

The doorbell chimed.

Kari shrieked with frustration. Tony groaned his disappointment.

They shared a speaking glance, burst out laughing, then quickly threw on their robes and went down the stairs.

Kari peered over Tony's shoulder as he pulled open the door to find a group of forty or so people standing behind Aridell Henderson Jones.

"We just came to talk." She lifted an eyebrow, taking in their disheveled appearance with a quick onceover, cleared her throat and added, "But if it's not a good time, we can come back a little later. Maybe much later—like tomorrow."

Tony looked at Kari, who sighed. "Now is as good a time as any," he said, inviting them in.

The group, made up of the choir, musicians, a few members, Ricky and an usher board member, filed into the living room, each greeting Tony and Kari as they walked past.

"Would you like for us to fix some beverages and refreshments for everyone?" Sister Janice asked and waited for Kari's nod before she, Sisters Susan, Martha, and Lorna went into the kitchen.

Aridell grinned, then leaned in so only Tony and Kari could hear. "Looks like y'all worked things out pretty well." She winked, then gave them an ear-to-ear grin. "I'm proud of you."

Kari felt her cheeks heat up. Tony had the nerve to look chagrinned.

Hushed whispers of conversation ensued while the men brought in chairs from the dining room, patio, garden, and the family room to accommodate the guests. Tony and Kari went upstairs to change with a humored warning from Sister Aridell. "Remember y'all got guests down here."

Kari gasped. "Sister Aridell—"

She ducked her head and tried not to laugh. "Y'all remind me of me and Richard. God knows I loved that man so much. Maybe too much," she said, sobering a little. "Probably asked God to take him before I wore him out."

"Lord have mercy," Kari said, placing a hand over her heart before following a laughing Tony up the stairs. "Don't encourage her, Tony."

That only made him laugh harder.

They came down about ten minutes later and Sister Aridell tapped an imaginary watch and grinned. Kari gave her the side eye as she took the seat that Sister Karen offered.

"We want to apologize to the first lady," Brother Michael said, his robust frame inching further into Sister Anita's space than she probably would like.

All around the room the rest of the members echoed those sentiments.

"I'm not the first lady any longer," Kari said, folding her arms over her full breasts.

"You're *our* first lady," Aridell corrected. "No matter what my knucklehead nephew has in mind." She put her gaze on Tony. "I've set a church meeting for Wednesday. The whole congregation will be there to get our new marching orders." She gestured to the people around the room. "This will be your new board, if you'll have us."

Tony perched on the edge of the sofa, the only available space in his home. He took in the expectant and eager expressions of those around him. "I know this isn't going to be what you want to hear, but after everything that went down today, I'm not trading one noose for one of my own making." He glanced at Kari, who nodded. "I was just having a talk with my wife and saying that a street ministry is what we're aiming for. So I won't be needing a board. Advisors, yes. A board, no. I'm not going to answer to anyone but God, my wife, and the government."

Silence greeted that.

"That's fair," Aridell said after a few moments, and there was an unmistakable disappointment in those two words.

Tony grinned at his new advisors. "I will say that you're a heck of a sight better than a board that's no more than a retired bunch of Negroes with more time on their hands than good sense."

The doorbell rang again.

"Who in the world could that be?" Kari said as she went to the door with Tony fast on her heels.

Lisa, Tee, and Cathy Henderson were on the porch.

Aridell came up beside Tony and Kari, her mouth tightened and expression went hard. "Well, butter my butt and call me a biscuit. Look who's here."

"You've got jokes," Tee said in a small voice. "We need to talk with Pastor Kimbrough."

"Shouldn't you be with Terrance," Aridell taunted. "Since your side of the family's trying to take over?"

"I didn't have nothing to do with that," Tee insisted, with a wary glance at Tony. "I'm not down with whatever they've got going on. I want to talk with pastor and you, Aunt Aridell."

Aridell's brown eyes narrowed on her grandniece. "Well, it's a little interesting that you showed up now, just when those of us supporting pastor are having a private meeting with him." She cocked her head at the other two women. "And don't think we didn't notice that neither of you stated your stance on what happened at the church."

"Come on in and take a seat," Kari offered, her tone not completely welcoming, but not exactly forbidding either.

"No, put them in the basement somewhere until our meeting's over," Aridell warned, keeping an eye on her family. "We don't want them taking any information back to the other side."

"We're not going to do that," Tony said, also keeping his focus on the three newcomers. "Unless they give us a reason not to trust them."

He went back into the living room to join the others spread out between the living room, dining room, kitchen and some in the solarium, all of whom shifted their gazes to the trio. Some quickly averted their gazes and whispered to the person next to them; others gave them a hard stare, a final few just shook their heads.

"Nothing's going on here that won't be public knowledge at some point," Tony said.

Aridell looked to Kari, who signaled for Aridell to be cool. But the older woman still wasn't feeling the love. She moved past all of them and reclaimed the seat she'd vacated, grumbling a few choice words along the way.

"Today was a turning point, and it brought home many things," Tony said to everyone. "This issue with the Henderson family has been brewing for a while, and the fact that the board and the deacons were all in on what he planned to do to my wife says that I'm not as good a judge of character as I thought."

"Naw, that wasn't it," Sister Mae said, her weathered hand dismissing his last words. "You'd have to have a different kind of radar to sniff out their kind of mess."

Everyone laughed. Even Sister Aridell. Well, except two of the three newcomers.

Tony left his seat, stood in the center of the living room at an angle where those in the other rooms could see him as well. "I've spent the last two years battling the people who don't see that the church is no good if it's not serving the people of the community. The church is all about people in need. I'm not going to forget that again."

"And we're with you on doing more community service," Sister Sandra offered, amidst verbal agreement from the rest of the people in the room. "My son was shot right in front of our house. He was home from college, just catching up with some of the family he hadn't seen in a while." She paused; her bottom lip trembled in an effort not to cry. Sister Aridell stroked a comforting hand across the stout woman's back. "They shot him. He wasn't in no gang or nothing like that. He was making good grades; wanted to be an engineer. They ended all that." She locked a tearful gaze with Tony as she said, "They're getting bolder every day. Every. Single. Day. The police ... they're always somewhere else when the shooting happens."

"Yet, when that officer shot that unarmed dude in the middle of the block," Sister Sharon said. "There were at least fifteen police cars and twice as many officers on one street."

Brother Ray leaned forward, resting his elbows on his knees. "How can we live six blocks from one of the largest police stations in the city, and have more shooting and crimes than the rest of Chicago combined?"

"How exactly do you think we can help, pastor?" Brother Thomas asked, rubbing a hand through his barely-there hair. "He's right, you know."

Tony shared a glance with Kari and said, "Tomorrow we're going to start off our search for a basic building that has offices."

"I have a spot about a block away from the church," Brother Ray said, sliding back comfortably on the sofa. "Closed on it last month. You said we should be buying property near the church, trying to put some life back into the area. My cleaning crew's going through it and it's nearly ready for me to rent. I can donate the space for your ministry's use. It'll be a tax write-off."

"That's awesome," Tony said, smiling at the stocky man. "And that's what I call a ram in the bush."

A few people smiled; some applauded. Brother Ray beamed.

"And when we finally have a building that might be used for a Sunday gathering, the members aren't going to just sit in positions and hold ground," Tony said, eyeing each of them. "Every ministry will serve a purpose inside and outside of those four walls. For instance …" He put his focus on Brother Ray, the only member present that represented the ushers. "The usher board will serve on Sunday mornings, but they'll also be the people who keep in touch with our visitors after they leave our service."

Tony shifted, placed a hand on Sister Sara's shoulder. "The nurse's board needs to be made up of real nurses who will head up fitness and nutrition training for the members as well as consistent visits to the sick and the shut-ins."

He swept a gaze across the silent people in the room. Then he went on to explain a little of the concept of people with professional degrees and experience being put to service in their field, in small ways so that it's spread out amongst several members. Which meant a lot of people, doing a small amount really well—and gaining more experience and references within the church.

"We're giving people something to do so they can put their salvation on wheels. Y'all still down with me on that?"

"That's so freaking awesome," Ricky said, beaming. "Can I head up the technology board?"

"There's no such thing as a technology board at a church," Sister Martha said, giving him a stern look that made him wither a little.

Tony ruffled the lad's unruly curls and said, "We do now. Everyone could learn their way around a computer."

"And how Facebook works, too," Aridell said with a smile at Lisa, Tee, and Cathy. "Teach them about those ally-rhythms and such."

"Algorithms," the teen and everyone else corrected.

"You know what I meant," Aridell grumbled.

Tony took some time to explain a few of the other systems he wanted in place, and the fact that in addition to a focus on women and girls who were victims of child sex-trafficking or sexual abuse, he was going to have Kari work on a limited basis with Aridell on the teen division.

"Me?" Kari said, looking at him for a long moment.

He nodded, gesturing for her to take the floor. "The perfect place to stop some of our youth from answering the call of the streets is at the beginning. Tell them what you told me."

Kari crossed one leg over the other. "When you give teens something to do, show them the finish line—take them on college tours, travel to other cities, maybe even to other countries—they realize that there are more important things to do in life than drugs, sex, and losing sight of their dreams." She paused long enough to see the expressions of admiration from everyone. "My thing is to keep them busy, keep them traveling, keep showing them that when they become adults, that's when the fun is supposed to start. That they'll have a bit more life if they don't have to worry about raising a child when they haven't finished being raised themselves." Kari looked at Aridell, who gave her a reassuring smile. "Or end up in rehab trying to shake addictions that should never have been theirs to begin with. Or be easily led into things that they shouldn't; by listening to someone making all kind of empty promises just to get between their legs."

"That certainly would've helped me," Tee admitted in a soft voice, referring to the fact she now had two children, suffered the loss of a third, no husband, and had problems trying to finish school and juggle work too.

"Indeed," Aridell said with a small smile in her grandniece's direction. "An idle mind is the Devil's playground. But it doesn't mean that you're not able to bounce back and do what you want to do in life. It just means it might take a little bit longer. You don't give up."

Tee nodded, and her eyes glazed over and then the tears streamed down her face.

Aridell moved in, pulling the young woman to her in an embrace.

Soon others were tearing up as well.

"I think I've always been jealous," Tee admitted.

Aridell pulled away to look at her. "Of what?"

"You helped Jennifer, Marco, and Malcolm through college," she said, her tone accusatory and angry. Then it turned soft and whiny. "But you didn't help me."

"Oh, sweetheart, that's what I would've done for you," Aridell said, cupping her hands around Tee's tear-stained face. "That's *exactly* what I wanted for you. Finish high school. College. A career. A life."

"But why did I have to sign that thing to get it?"

"Because you needed some type of boundaries," Aridell replied, flickering a gaze at Cathy, who seemed sad for some reason. "Your cousins did, too. Putting it in writing makes sure that everybody knows what's what. It's giving you some clear rules and direction. That's all." She looked at Cathy. "I wasn't trying to take your child away like you said. I wanted better for her than what you were able to give back then."

Tee's gaze landed on her mother then shifted to Kari, who tried to offer a smile of encouragement.

"I'm sorry, Auntie," Tee whispered, flexing her hands, a sure sign that her emotions were running high. "I'm really, really sorry."

Aridell nodded, then spread her arms and the girl came forward into another embrace.

Though Kari was warmed by the reunion, and so were others, she scanned the group until she looked into Lisa's eyes and the animosity was so strong it was able to reach across the room and choke out all of the happiness that the niece and aunt shared.

Aridell kept her arm about her niece's shoulders as she moved them both into the middle of the living room. "This new direction that Pastor Kimbrough wants to take the church in is something that we're all in agreement with."

"Amen."

"Yes."

"Of course."

"Did you keep a copy of the church records, Pastor?" Ricky asked, causing Tony to glance in his direction.

"No paper files, but all the documents were scanned to a system and they're kept on a special hard drive."

"Encrypted?"

"All of them," Tony asked, his gaze narrowing on him. "At church and right here. What does that matter?"

"Someone in as much of a hurry to get their hands on the church as Minister Henderson is, might have some other ideas, like signing your name to something or printing out a document and backdating it."

Half the people in the room looked shocked.

"You watch way too much television," Lisa grumbled, pressing her back to the entrance between the rooms.

Kari looked to her husband. "And there's all of those confidential records you created when you became pastor. They contain financial information and even personal things you may have written down during counseling sessions. He's right. They shouldn't be in just anyone's hands." She crossed the room and placed her hands flat against his chest. "If Henderson was keyed up enough to go behind your back and get the board and deacons to saddle up and ride to his cause, then he won't be above using any of that information for his own needs."

"My brother wouldn't do that," Lisa snapped, her expression filled with animosity as she glared at Kari.

Everyone's gaze shifted to Lisa, whose lips were set in a thin, disapproving line.

"Care to share why after several months you showed up at church today?" Kari asked, undeterred by the woman's demeanor. "And why you're really here, in my home, right now?"

Tee and her mother shared a glance, but it was Cathy who seemed suddenly uncomfortable.

"I wanted to have a talk with Pastor to resolve this issue with Aridell," she defended, chest puffing up a little.

Aridell scoffed, but remained silent when Tony shot her a warning glance.

"So instead of calling to set up a meeting at a later time," Kari reasoned, getting to her feet. "You just showed up here when you knew all of these people were coming this way?"

Aridell cleared her throat, and put a warning glance to Tony that said, "You'd better listen to your wife."

"I'll give you the information you need right now to make all that information secure on my computer," Tony said to Ricky while scribbling on a sheet of paper that Brother Ray gave him. "Snatch the files labeled counseling from the church's computer and place it on this cloud account, then make a backup on the hard drive that I have here."

"What about the financial records?" Ricky said, accepting the document.

"Legally, the church records, finances, board meeting minutes should remain. They're the property of the church. I have a copy here just in case they decide to do some creative accounting of their own and try to pawn it off on me. Good looking out, little man."

"Sure thing, Pastor," the teen said, taking the slip of paper Tony held out to him.

"The computer's upstairs in the last room on the left."

Ricky made it to the stairs and froze.

"Nothing else on it that I shouldn't see, right? I mean ..." He looked over his shoulder, giving a quick, sheepish look at Kari, then back to Tony so they'd take his meaning.

"No!!" Tony and Kari yelled.

"I don't know, Pastor," Aridell teased with a suggestive lift of her eyebrows. "You and Sister Kari seem awfully happy these days."

"Doesn't mean we're putting it on video, though," Tony said as Kari shook her head.

While the rest of the people shared a laugh, Tony jerked his thumb toward the upper level and the teen scrambled up the stairs.

"Then it's settled," Aridell said, allowing a smile to grace her lips. "On Wednesday we let the rest of the church know what's what. Either they're riding with you, or they're rolling with the imposter."

A round of applause followed.

Kari didn't fail to notice that Tee was all smiles and her hands were still placed in Aridell's, but Lisa and Cathy were the last to join in.

Chapter 13

Kari settled into the passenger seat of their silver Buick LaCrosse as Tony maneuvered down I-57. A sense of foreboding filled her for no reason she could name. Over the past three days, she'd taken off work to spend time with him as they talked extensively about their past, their marriage and their personal goals. The more she spoke of having a focus on sexual abuse and child trafficking victims, the more she realized that she might have to delegate more responsibility of the daily operations of her business to someone else. She recently signed a contract with a firm to provide more well-trained staff for a civil case. But in order to give the new ministery, and her husband, the full attention they deserved-- she didn't want to split her focus.

"You know," Tony said. "Each one of the choir members contacted me, letting me know they're with me all the way."

"Well, isn't there a saying that you've been preaching to the choir? Maybe they, Aridell, the advisors, and little Ricky are the only ones who've been listening."

Tony chuckled, saying, "With them added in, that makes fifty percent of the church membership that wants to roll with us."

"Fifty percent? That's a lot more than the ten you started with.

Sounds like God's trying to tell you something."

Tony gave her the side-eye at her reference to the song from the movie *The Color Purple*, but didn't bother to hide a smile.

For a moment, she closed her eyes, tried to clear her mind and prepare for a meeting that was sure to be interesting at best. She had not realized how much weight holding her secret had carried.

Minutes later, Kari felt Tony's tension and opened her eyes to see what had caused the change.

The street leading up to the church lot was filled with an extraordinary amount of cars, news vans, and crowds of people milling about. They had to park a block away, then looped their way through the onlookers and the church members who were watching a heated exchange between the old board members and deacons and Tony's advisors.

Cameras were rolling, picking up every word. Even the tad bit profane ones—none of which were in the Bible—spewing from the old guard.

Kari noted that Aridell and the advisors presented a calm, united front. The others—Henderson's people—had spread out in front of the church doors, blocking the path of anyone who wanted to enter. Their anger was evident in their contorted faces, rants, and fists shaking in the air. None of this put the church in the best light. How in the world had it come to this? And who had invited the press? Certainly no one in their camp would want outsiders to have a front seat to church dissension. This reeked of Henderson's showboating.

She peered between that sliver of space between Brothers Philip and Derrick to find a huge padlock and massive silver chain hooked between the handles of the solid oak entry doors. More than likely they were on the back and side doors as well, otherwise Aridell and the advisors would already be inside.

Henderson's pompous self was off to the side holding court with a band of reporters. Microphones thrust outward, they gave him their rapt attention, soaking up whatever drivel he had to impart. None of it would be favorable to her husband, Sister Aridell, or the advisors.

"Looks like there's a welcoming party," she said to Tony.

"And we're not welcome."

Tony held out his hands and she slipped hers inside. He edged through the crowd, creating a path to the front door where his people stood firm. The choir members and musicians had sorrowful expressions at seeing this play out in such a public manner; the others were cheering Henderson on.

"The majority of the congregation has signed this petition for dismissal," Henderson said to the reporters. "We now have control of the church."

More like only fifty percent. Kari glanced up at Tony. She recognized the flickering movements beneath his lowered lids. He was praying for peace—probably his own.

When he opened his eyes and scanned the cameras, a couple of the reporters shot their focus his way.

"Sweetheart, why don't you go on home," he said.

Even now, instead of letting loose with what he really wanted to say, he was concerned that this would come back on her somehow. But she couldn't let him face this alone. They were a team, and part of the reason this was happening right now was because she hadn't been strong enough to tell him or to tell her truth to the congregation just like he had on day one.

"If you're going in, so am I," she replied, putting a tighter grip on his hand. "I'm not much of a fighter, but if you hold them down, I'll poke 'em in the eye real hard."

That statement gained a smile, then outright laughter from him.

"And there he is," another long-lost member of Henderson's family standing near the door said, her lips twisted in a sneer.

Nearly all eyes shifted in their direction.

The crowd parted, allowing enough space for Kari and Tony to move forward to Henderson, who stood grinning at them as though he'd hit the lottery.

Maybe he had. Through subterfuge, deception and total disregard for the written bylaws, he'd stolen a church without even so much as the church membership approving. Henderson had a sense of entitlement from having come from a long line of pastors—some good, some bad. And not one of them had what it took to expand the church's reach and membership the way Tony had. None of them had his vision.

Tony's sermons weren't those fiery, guilt-laden types that she remembered growing up. Instead, they were filled with humor, stories from the Bible with a current day slant and thought provoking questions that some were encouraged to stand and answer during service. His lessons were interactive and engaging. He wanted to teach the members how to lead, not just follow.

Truthfully, she'd been more of a follower. The minute she and Tony had walked through those doors, they found countless women vying to take over positions that the former first lady held. For that, Kari was grateful. Until she realized that the position nearly half of them wanted was in her husband's bed.

Kari trusted Tony, and that was saying a lot for a woman who didn't give it easily. But she knew better than to trust any woman chasing after her husband. Aridell had handled the more aggressive ones who didn't catch any of Tony's outright hints that he wouldn't betray his wife. Thankfully, Kari never had to have what Aridell called a "Come to Jesus" meeting to set them straight. If she had, it would have been more like a "Calling on Jesus" meeting. And she wouldn't have been the one on the main line.

Henderson cast a mocking glance in Kari's direction. "Now this is the real story right here. Pastor Kimbrough's *wife*." The once-over that slid down Kari's body sent a shiver of disgust through her.

"You leave my wife out of it," Tony said through his teeth.

"I assume every one of y'all want to tell your viewers the God-honest truth," Aridell said, eyeing the flock of reporters like they were a bunch of unruly kids getting a mother's verbal reprimand before she took things to the next level. She came over to stand with Kari and Tony, and pointed at him. "This pastor right here wants to make a difference in this community. Same difference as he's made in the church."

She angled so that all of the cameras had a clear view. "This church is finally debt free. Some of the members of the congregation are debt free. All the property this church owns," she said, gesturing to the park directly next to the church building. "All the services we offer, *he* made that happen."

"We've sent children to college on full scholarships. Put mentoring programs in place for children who don't have fathers in their lives."

Tony held up his hands in a gesture for her to tone it down a bit.

Instead, she ignored him and cranked it up. "He wants to take on some of the issues that are making Chicago so unsafe."

"You're taking on the gangs?" one red-haired reporter asked, pushing the microphone further in Aridell's direction.

"We're taking on the gangs *and* the police," she shot back, putting up an index finger. "Both of them are shooting at folks with no clear direction these days. And innocent folks are paying the price. Children on their porches, on the way to school." She put a glare in Henderson's direction. "He and those people standing with him don't want this church to get involved. God didn't tell us to hide our light under a bushel. But if they have their way, the church's light will go out completely."

"She's dancing around the real issue," Henderson said with another side-glance in Kari's direction. "Our real problem is that we need fine, upstanding people at the head of this church. People who don't have criminal records or ... *questionable* backgrounds."

The media's movements seemed more suited to a synchronized swimming team. All heads, cameras, and microphones shifted in Tony's direction.

"I have a past, and I let the church know it coming through the door. But that didn't have anything to do with how I've run this church." Tony released Kari's hand and moved to a space where all the cameras were on him. "And I'm willing to open the books to the church members *and* the public to prove it."

"We have a board in place, and they want him gone," Henderson said, holding up the petition. "This church has been under the direction of a Henderson for many years and it needs to return to the family fold."

"So he's misappropriated church funds?" one buxom reporter asked, shoving a microphone further towards Henderson's mouth.

"We're looking into all that," Henderson mumbled.

"What for?" Aridell's voice rang out over the thrum of conversation taking place among the rest of the congregation and the neighbors who had spilled out from their homes to watch the fireworks. "The man just said he'd open up the financial records to the public," she challenged. "You need to be honest about the reason you want to take over this church, *Minister* Henderson. It's not because Pastor Kimbrough isn't doing a good job, it's because you need the income and the board wants to keep dipping its hand in the pot.

Applause rang out from Tony's people.

"Pastor Kimbrough demanded some changes in the administration," Aridell explained. "And some of those board members are ticked off because they're no longer over the finances. Now they can't take all those trips and charge it to the church."

"Just curious," Tony said to the reporters. "How is it that every news station in Chicago has someone here today, but not a single one showed up to do a story when our secretary sent a press release about our mentoring program and the scholarships we offer?"

"News desk hotline," one said and had the nerve to look embarrassed.

Another said, "We received a notice of a press conference because the members were locking the doors to keep the pastor out."

"And you came for that?" Tony said with a wry twist of his lips. "Must be a slow news day."

Kari gave Tony's jacket a little yank to get his attention. "Don't antagonize them. It's obvious that what we hoped to accomplish here won't happen today. Judging by the looks of things, it won't happen at all," she said with a nod at the congregation cheering for Henderson.

Tony looped his arm under Kari's, moved forward and hooked his other arm under Aridell's and guided them away from the cameras. He signaled the rest of the advisors, musicians, Ricky, and the choir to follow. When they made it far enough away, which happened to be near the corner grocery store, everyone circled him.

"Pastor, we need to reschedule and come back another time," Brother

Ray said, looking over his shoulder at the people who were now filing away from the front of the church, small groups at a time.

"Why?" Aridell asked. "The doors are going to be locked every time we show up." She nudged Tony. "No time like the present. Go out there. Speak your real agenda while the cameras are rolling and let Henderson try to come for you after that."

"I'm with Aridell," Sister Janice said, with a nod that said *that settles it*. "Tell the media all those good things you've been doing. That'll get the right people in your favor."

"I don't have to broadcast that to anyone," he said, giving her shoulder a pat. "It wasn't done so the world or anyone else could give me any kind of credit." He followed her gaze to the front doors of the church; the chain glittering under the glare of the street lights. "I'm not letting this play out in the media. Church is already getting enough bad press, pastors, too. I'm not adding to it."

Tony was right. One pastor from across town had already been under fire for pocketing money while several female members put their own money up just to keep the church's lights and gas on. Then he made up some lies about those same members and banned them from the church. Another pastor who impregnated one of the pre-teens from his congregation was currently up on charges of sexual assault of a minor. Not to mention the one who'd been having an affair with the former choir director. Both were married. Oh, and male.

"We'll just meet at my house next Sunday, he said to the group. "Agreed?"

Everyone nodded, and everyone came forward one by one to shake Tony's hand.

Henderson walked past the group on the way to his vehicle.

"You want this place that bad," Tony stated, "then it's all yours. Same way that God led me here, He'll use these same feet and walk me to the next opportunity."

Kari chanced a glance at their nemesis and was met with an expression that was pure evil.

Chapter 14

As the media circus followed behind Henderson and his people, Aridell moseyed over to her nephew and said, "Youngster, you're about to learn the difference between tithers and tippers."

"What's that supposed to mean?"

She dismissed him with an airy wave. "The church needs a certain amount of prayer, manpower, and money to run. Folks who volunteer their time do a lot of things around here. But there are certain paid positions, like minister of music or assistant pastor," Aridell explained. "You've got to make sure *they* get paid, as well as keep the gas, lights and telephone on, and pay for insurance, all of that. And of course *you're* going to want money to live on."

Henderson laughed, eyes crinkling with the effort. "I have the majority of the congregation with me. We're going to be all right."

Aridell smiled as she peered around him to the people watching them closely. "There are people who ask God for things all the time, but when it's time to give Him one of the things He asks, they put a drop in the offering bucket. Those are the tippers. Then there are tithers like me, who give God ten percent off the top, give themselves that second ten percent, and still drop God a little something extra."

She waited while her meaning caught on. "The group that's backing Pastor Kimbrough? Those are the tithers." She gave him a wink. "I give it three months tops before you're in financial trouble. Real trouble. Not to mention, if they did a little digging in your past, then the media will have a whole new story."

The smile that had been ever-present on Henderson's lips since the media had landed on the church's doorstep disappeared, replaced by panic. As he put his eyes on the part of the congregation that were sprawled out over the block, Aridell gave him a parting wave and turned on her heels.

On the way home from church, Tony and Kari both were bombarded with texts, emails and calls from some of the former members; ones that had not been on Tony's side.

"Maybe we should give them another chance," Kari said after a few moments. "It seems they're having second, possibly third, thoughts.

Tony glanced at her from the driver's seat. "Kari, we're fighting a battle that the majority of those folks don't want us to win. We don't need lukewarm members who keep swaying from one side to the other. We want people to think; to explore; to know God for themselves and know what's right."

"I understand all that," she countered, placing a hand to his cheek. "But you've put so much time and money into that place. They're finally coming around."

"I don't need them to come around," he replied in a low tone. "They can stay right where they're comfortable. The ones who sided with Henderson are the very ones who'll be the first to judge the kind of people we'll be bringing in. And I'm going to be honest with you." He took his hand off the steering wheel and placed it on her thigh. "They'll be the first ones to open their mouths to say something to you on the sly. And I'm certainly not going to let that happen."

"I'm a lot tougher than you think," she countered. "There's going to be some times when you won't be able to protect me, Tony. You'll have to accept that. I've been hiding behind you for far too long." She chanced a glance his way, wondering if dropping a little more information on him would be a good thing. "And Tony, I have to be honest about something else. I don't believe in God the way Sister Aridell or Brother Ray does; the way *you* do. I've always had issues with religion, with doctrine that seems to limit the value of women. How am I supposed to adore a God who allows such mistreatment of women as rape and torture? And this whole thing we're going through with the church only adds to it. It's hard to believe in God when I keep seeing nothing but ugliness in the world."

Kari was silent for a few moments, waiting to see his reaction—which was only the flicker of his eyes, meaning he was processing and thinking of a response. A response that was not immediate in coming.

"I've always done what it takes to support you as my husband, but … I've never felt what you feel. I've wanted it, but it's never been like that for me. You're so passionate about this; about life. I see that how you teach changes people, and they get all caught up in the Spirit, but that's not me. I'm an imperfect Christian, if I'm truly a Christian at all."

"But that's what God uses—imperfect people," he said, setting his gaze on her for a few seconds before putting his focus on the traffic again. "I never asked you to be perfect. I'm not perfect. I live with the mistakes I've made on a daily basis."

Those words swirled around for a long while before he said, "You didn't sign up for any of this."

"Of course I did," she shot back. "You never kept it a secret that you were going to take this path. I could've left long before we got in so deep."

"It was deep from day one," he said, the corners of his lips lifting a little.

"You will be extremely happy some things didn't work out like you once wanted them to. God's plans can, and will, exceed your dreams and desires." – Pastor Karen Williams

Chapter 15

The next morning, Tony was looking down at Kari when she awoke. The minute her eyes focused he said, "Get dressed, baby. I want to take you someplace."

She reached up to stroke his smooth skin, the color of pure milk chocolate. "And you're not going to tell me where?"

"Nope." He smiled, showing those perfect white teeth and her heart did a little flip.

"I don't know if I'm liking this mysterious side of you."

"Good," he said, nuzzling her neck. "Don't want you to think you have me all figured out."

"Should I be worried?"

"Not about us," he replied, sliding a hand across the smooth expanse of exposed skin. "Never about us."

An hour later they were on Lake Shore Drive, headed toward the museum campus. They parked in a lot adjacent to a stone building with a dome layered in green shades.

"The Adler Planetarium?" she asked, following him up the steps to the entrance. "Some date this is." Despite what she said earlier, she was loving his mysterious vibe.

Tony chuckled. "It's not just a date. I'm trying to prove a point, love."

They walked a short distance to the desk, where he asked the busty woman behind the counter for two tickets to see Cosmic Wonder. Then they were directed to a theatre and he chose two seats in the rear away from the others so they would have a bit of privacy.

The narrated show began with a vivid and astounding display of the Earth, showing where it stood in relation to the other planets and the sun. It soon zoomed out to the Milky Way and the nearest galaxy.

"You see that?" he whispered after a few moments.

Kari nodded, still not certain if she understood any of the points he was trying to get across with this visit. Part of their world had come to a screeching halt and he wanted to look at planets and stars?

"See where earth is?" Tony asked.

Then the image zoomed out more, showing the entire expanse of a galaxy, followed by another, and yet another. It made everything beyond Earth's realm seem … endless. In that moment, she felt small in the scheme of things. Kari tried to keep up with the fast-moving visuals, but her mind was going at its own speed.

Was there life on other planets? Were the people like us? Do they believe in the same God? Do they have the same issues on their planets as we have on Earth?

Tony smiled as he watched her. "God is so much more than what we see," he whispered.

Now she understood why he brought her here.

She had never given any real thought to the magnificent labor that went into creating this planet, this universe, and so many others. It was as much an intricate work as the creation of the human body.

So many systems had to work together in perfect harmony to keep a person breathing, living, walking, talking, thinking and growing. What a wonderful thing that was. Like human beings. Each person a system within a system, some parts of it good, other parts …

"It's beautiful," she said in a voice just above a whisper. "Awesome in fact. But how can God be powerful enough to do all of this, yet not able to erase sin and human cruelty that has existed for ages?" She took a long slow breath and let it out slowly.

He reached for her hands. "I understand why you would only see God as a punisher. But that's not who He is." Tony paused a moment before continuing, "Consider this. I've known you for years and still don't know everything there is to know about you, right?"

She nodded.

"I can only hope to know the most important parts you share with me," he said in a tone just above a whisper. "It's the same with God. There's no way that I, or any other finite person, can fully understand everything about God and how He operates. But He reveals parts of Himself to me when I pray, or when I study the Bible. And He is so much more than anything man has ever written and re-written about Him."

She couldn't help the smile that came. "You're so smart. That's why you need to keep teaching people about God." Her smile disappeared and she peered at him. "How did you ever end up in that drug life in the first place, sweetheart?"

Tony raised his gaze to the ceiling where the display of galaxies, purples, whites, and blacks was nothing short of breathtaking. "I was running from the calling a minister said I had on my life. I was twelve when he said that to me. My grandparents dragged me into church that Sunday. I didn't want to be responsible for people like that. After that I didn't go back to church."

Then his life took an ugly turn. Tony's brother, Damon, skipped out on that last two years of high school and managed to get into Malik Price for twenty large. Malik, a man who'd been in the drug trade since age twelve, didn't play about his cash, and Damon, who'd been ducking him for weeks, was about to see the wrong side of the grave.

A single bullet to the leg served enough of a warning where Damon left Chicago for parts unknown. Unfortunately, Malik knew exactly where Damon's family lived and came to have a not quite friendly little chat with the family, bodyguards in tow, demanding his money—in either cash or service.

Tony's mother, Ruth, had been a praying woman. She had more faith in God to protect their family, than in Malik's ability to kill them. Tony was the exact opposite. He, and everyone else, was well aware of Malik's handiwork and he wasn't going to attend one funeral after another until the man had made his point. Money or service.

Ruth had worked two jobs to keep their family afloat. Three daughters and two sons, and a small wooden house that was barely enough space for all of them. Only one of her children had been pulled by the call of the streets. The others had excelled in school and went on to find their success. One became a doctor of optometry, another a human resources administrator, and a third a social worker.

But back then, Tony didn't trust God where Malik was concerned. He didn't trust the police either, who were too busy doing their part to make sure that the addict-dealer-prison drug triangle continued. Tony recognized straight out of the gate that if the drug trade ended, then one of the police's reason for getting paid would come to a screeching halt. He learned that police were simply generating revenue and feeding a pipeline of bodies to the prison system--owned by people making a profit off that kind of labor.

So instead of Tony making that trip to Washington, D.C. and taking his place among the freshman class beginning their first semester at Howard University, he was posted up on the corners doing "service". Time on the streets meant selling the kind of poison that separated users from reality; mothers from children; families from people they no longer recognized as human.

"So God sat me down in that jail and took away all outside distractions. I had no other choice but to listen." Tony laced his fingers with hers. "One thing I learned is that for some, there's no such thing as rehabilitation in prison—most inmates spend their sentences learning how to be better criminals."

"Except you."

"Except me," he agreed. "And a few others."

"My first night in lock-up, my cellmate tried to test me because I didn't have the protection that so many others had coming into the joint. Prison has its own system, and the warden and guards can't be everywhere at once. The inmates know it and use it to their advantage."

Tony put his focus upward to take in the transformation of the milky way projected onto the ceiling. "My cell mate didn't know me from Adam, and I had no beef with him. But he came at me with a homemade knife just the same. His intentions weren't actually to kill me."

Kari shut her eyes against the image that came to mind. Yet another type of cruelty that was unexplainable.

"I had to send a message that I wasn't the one to try," Tony explained. "When they pulled me off of him, he had to be airlifted to the nearest hospital. I didn't have any more problems with anyone after that." He looked at Kari for a long moment and when she didn't respond, he listened to a bit of the show's narrative.

"I wasn't proud of what I'd done. But I did what I had to do so I could live to see the day I'd get out of that place," Tony said, shifting his gaze from the screen to Kari. "There was this older guy who'd been there for a little while. And I saw something so different about him. The way he handled himself and handled others ..." Tony shifted downward in the chair, long legs angling for more space. "I hadn't seen anything like it. People listened to him. Looked up to him. Respected him. He wasn't the type of Christian that was praying all the time or spitting Bible verses with every other sentence. He lived his faith, even in a place as dark as that."

Tony was silent, as though he had journeyed back to that time. The mustard seed of faith shown by that one man had sparked a passion for knowledge within Tony, enough to make a bad boy from the West side of Chicago seek God in a way that had a life-altering impact on him and indirectly on others. With all she'd learned from Tony's teachings over the years, it was a wonder that she had any doubts at all.

"When I was released … that was the true test of my faith," he said. "Malik still wanted that service, though it was the very thing that landed me behind bars." Tony chanced a look at Kari. "I held my ground on not getting back into that life. I had to believe that God would allow me to stay alive to keep my word to Him. When you stare down the business end of a nine millimeter and come out on the living side, you have to believe there's a God somewhere."

Kari was silent for a few moments then locked a gaze on him. "You should've married a first lady who you'd be more equally yoked with."

"I married a woman who would balance me and keep me grounded," he countered, as though none of her concerns mattered. "And questioning God isn't a reason for you to leave me. Everyone questions God at one time or another." Then he grinned. "Now if you tell me you're voting for Trump, then yeah, *that* might be grounds for an immediate divorce."

Kari couldn't help the laugh that bubbled over.

He joined in, and the people seated twelve rows in front of them looked their way to silence them.

"Nothing about my life has ever been normal," he admitted in a whisper. "Yours either. That's why we fit. We don't have any unrealistic expectations." He stroked a gentle hand across her face. She kissed the open palm, eliciting a smile.

"I never wanted you to be vulnerable because of me," she said, looking into the depths of those green eyes that sparkled even in the dim lighting of the theatre. "They came at you because of me."

"They came at me because they're greedy. Don't put this on yourself. We're about to come under some serious heat because of money, not you. Henderson and his family are coming with all weapons drawn. We need to be able to take a punch and give one back."

"We can't go blow for blow with them," she warned.

"Says who? God said the meek will inherit the earth, but He didn't say we had to just stand by and get our butts kicked in the process."

Kari looked at the people who were now filing out of the theatre. She thought about all that Tony had said. "I want to embrace that part of

God that is unlike what I experienced."

"I'm glad to hear that," Tony replied, stroking his thumb across her open palm. "People are quick to lay everything horrible that happens in this world at God's feet. They take Job's statement 'the Lord giveth and the Lord taketh away' as proof that God was the one who caused the horrible things that happened to Job. But that's a common misconception. If they would read the beginning, they'd see that it was Satan who caused Job to lose his children, his wealth, and his health. He hated Job with a passion because God said Job was a perfect and upright man. Satan was certain that losing everything would make Job curse God. But Job didn't curse God, and God gave back everything he lost and then some."

She laid her head on his chest, taking that in as the last of the group shot curious looks their way. Why did Tony make it all seem so simple, yet for her it was so hard?

Tony's focus remained on the white walls with shadows of personnel who were preparing the theatre for the next patrons.

"We can't even get earth right and yet we expect to fall all up into the VIP section of Heaven. But I want you to remember one thing ..."

She raised her head to look into his eyes.

"The visual of how the planets in our solar system all revolve around one thing."

Kari thought about that for a few second and said, "The sun. They all have their time in the sun."

Tony smiled and for moment she was able to push away the dark issue that eclipsed their world. "This is our time in the sun."

She could believe that, but in the darkest corner of her mind there was a whisper of doubt when it came to one person in particular.

"I don't think that Henderson is going to give up so easy."

"That's all right, sweetheart," he said placing a kiss on her temple. "We'll be ready for whatever he brings"

Chapter 16

Tony opened the front door of his home to find two suit-clad men on the other side of the threshold. The pale one narrowed his gaze as though sizing Tony up. The other, whose sienna complexion was several shades darker than Tony's, lifted an eyebrow. Probably expected the short, pot-bellied kind of pastor, rather than one whose physique was in better condition than his own. Even still, they reeked of law enforcement. The local kind. And that wasn't a good thing.

"What can I do for you, officers?"

"Detective Archer," the Black one said. "And Detective Donovan."

"What can I do for you, detectives?"

Donovan tried to peer over Tony's shoulder. "May we come in?"

"For?"

They both seemed taken aback by his response, but it was Archer who said, "We need to have a little chat."

"Chats only take a couple of minutes," Tony said with a mild shrug. "Wouldn't want you to get too comfortable."

The detectives shared a glance, then resigned themselves to being on the opposite side of the door. "There's been some allegations of theft of church property."

Well, that came out of left field. "I haven't been allowed into the building since I left on Sunday."

"They're talking records for the past three years," Donovan explained"They've all been wiped from the church's computer."

"Well, that could be a problem." Tony leaned his shoulder on the doorjamb, folding his arms over his massive chest, waiting.

"Lisa Henderson said that you had some teenager steal the files."

"He didn't steal anything. And if I did have him do anything then that would be a civil matter, not a police matter," Tony countered. "So, I'm still not sure why you're here."

The two men moved forward in an effort to intimidate Tony. After being housed with men who had killed people for something as simple as looking at them the wrong way, and the guards who had done things more criminal than the inmates, Tony's ability to be intimidated by anyone with a badge was slim to none.

"We were hoping that this could all be done peacefully," Archer said, angling his body so he had a clear view of one side of the street. "Seeing that your church has been all in the news these days, you don't need any more bad publicity."

"It's not my church anymore," Tony countered, keeping a keen eye on Archer who seemed mildly uncomfortable with being at Tony's place. "And the media being there wasn't my doing."

"Then releasing those records shouldn't be a problem," Donovan shot back. "This could all go away if you'd just give Terrance Henderson what he wants."

Tony thought that over for a minute and then narrowed his gaze on Archer once again; picking up on familiar features like that peanut-shaped head. A common trait of the males of one family in particular. Then it suddenly dawned on him that Archer was somehow related to the Henderson family. Henderson probably believed that a little police pressure would put some fear in Tony. Especially given his background.

Evidently, he didn't know Tony Kimbrough so well.

Now the reason for the officer's lack of a search warrant became clear. More than likely, they didn't have clearance to be here. This was a little off-duty, off-the-books work. Tony could call them on it, but what purpose would it serve? "Tell Mr. Henderson and his board that I will turn over all records at church this Sunday."

"And we'll have a few conditions," Kari said, coming forward to peer over Tony's shoulder.

When she shifted so the officers were able to get a better glance, both men suddenly seemed a lot less interested in church records, and a lot more interested in Tony's wife. Tony shifted his stance so that it blocked Kari from their view.

"If they have a problem with that," she continued. "Then everything will be settled in a court of law."

"It doesn't have to go that far," Archer said, scowling.

"Let's hope it doesn't," she said, putting a hand on Tony's arm, guiding him into the house and closing the door behind them.

"We'll tell them you said this Sunday," the detective said, loud enough to hear through the door.

Tony trailed Kari to the kitchen where breakfast was waiting.

"Are you sure about this?"

"They can have the church records," he said, claiming one of the high seats at the gathering table. "I can make all of that available to the public so they'll know that no shady business was going on. It's the others that I'm concerned about. If the *members* want their own record of giving and the records from their counseling sessions with me, I won't hold them." He grabbed up his cell and sent a quick text. "I'll have our resident techie put each one on a separate flash drive encrypted by the person's social security number. If they want Henderson to have it, then they can give it directly to him."

"Or not," Kari said, taking a sip of fresh squeezed orange juice.

"Or not," he agreed, placing a kiss on her lips.

"Nice of you to join us," Henderson said, not bothering to hide his sarcasm. He wore a custom tailored pinstriped suit that reeked of money. A fresh haircut and goatee trim tightened up the look he was going for—prosperous preacher man. "Do you have what we asked for?"

Tony gestured to the boxes he and each of his advisors held. He gave Aridell a warning look, his reminder for her to remain silent, as he had asked. But it was Kari who spoke to the Sunday congregation. "These boxes contain flash drives, and each of those flash drives contains your individual information. Everyone will get their own records tonight. We only ask that you sign one of these releases, verifying that you've received them. Once you get your records, if you choose to give them to someone else, that is certainly your right."

"That's not how it works," Henderson yelled, rushing forward to block them. "That's not what the agreement was."

"I didn't agree to anything with you," Tony said, focusing a hard gaze on the man. "You sent the police to retrieve them, I sent back a message that I'd release them on Sunday. I didn't say who I'd release them to." He lifted up a single drive with Henderson's name written in silver marker and placed it in his palm. "All the official church records, like minutes and finances, are on this one, as well as a record of your personal giving is. Everyone else will get a drive containing a record of their giving, and another drive if I have notes from any counseling I may have done with them. They can do with it what they will and can see everything was above board."

Some nodded, others verbally consented. None of it sat well with Henderson.

"I need to know *exactly* how much each member's supposed to be paying in tithes," Henderson protested. "Ten percent off the top before taxes."

Murmurs of discontent ripped through the church. Only the board and deacons seemed unbothered.

This was only a taste of what would come. Pastors like Henderson were not waiting for their cut any longer. Some even withheld help from members if their tithes weren't current.

"That's well and fine," Tony said, gesturing for Kari and his advisors to span out in front of the area leading to the pulpit. Each one held a sign that showed a range of alphabets.

Kari perched on the edge of the front pew, and gave a batch of papers and pens to the choir members who spread out over the rows behind her. "Take one and pass it back." She walked over to the other side and gave a stack to Sister Margaret, who slid one off the top, then passed the rest to the next person.

Kari said to everyone, "Please come and stand in front of the person who has the card that identifies the first letter of your last name."

"You can't just come in here and do this," Brother Samuel growled. "Give them to us, and we'll give them to the members after we've made the copies we need for our files."

"No," Sister Tracey said shaking her head as she maneuvered around him to get in line. "I don't want y'all to have my information. I think Pastor Kimbrough's way is best."

Several people agreed with her and soon the congregation was voicing their thoughts on the matter.

The first few people finished their forms, handed them to one of the advisors at the front of the church and accepted their flash drives, pocketing them and walking right past Henderson.

"How do we know that he doesn't have copies himself?" Brother Lawrence, one of the board members, asked. Though his dentures were having a hard time keeping up with his lips and words.

"All my backups on the computer and in the cloud were erased the moment we pulled these off," Tony shot back. "I'm starting my ministry from square one and building from there. I don't need these records. You do."

"You were aiming to turn this church into a social center," Henderson taunted, his gaze arrowed in on the people in line as though making a mental note of the names.

"Why shouldn't it be?" Tony asked. "There was a time when everything centered around the church. Maybe it should be that way again."

"Bid whist for couples?" Henderson scoffed with a dismissive wave. "Stepping lessons for singles?"

"If people want to live a little, have some fun, why can't the church provide a clean, safe environment for them to do so?" Tony said, putting his gaze on Kari before looking back at Henderson, who frowned at the lines of people getting their flash drives.

"I'm not going to be the kind of minister who's stuck in the old ways," Tony continued, drawing up the white covering from the communion table and shuddering at the fermented grape juice and stale crackers underneath. "This has been here all week? Nobody thought to … never mind."

Henderson glowered angrily at his wife, flickering his hand so that she hurried forward to remove the silver trays.

"I'm not focusing on doctrine or religion," Tony continued, causing a few heads to turn his way as they waited for their drives. "Jesus ticked folks off because he didn't do that either. He focused on the needs of the people and that's what brought them to God. I don't get caught up in that whole letter of the Biblical law thing—that was a Pharisee thing. I'm more about being in the Spirit of God. That's a Jesus thing. That dude right there was radical."

Tony moved up the aisle, all eyes on him. "There's a church on every street in Chicago, sometimes three on one block. Yet there's more crime, domestic violence, sexual abuse and assualt, teen pregnancy, divorces, and poverty than ever. We can't expect the government to take care of these problems. *We* have to do it for ourselves. And with God watching over us, that's exactly what we"—he gestured to his people— "are going to do." He turned to face Henderson. "We have to believe in a God that's more powerful than what's out there in streets. Either you believe and bring all you've got, or stay on the sidelines and out of our way."

"Sidelines sound about right," Deacon John grumbled, and the few people nearest him gave him the side-eye.

"Do you realize there's more people outside of church than in?" Tony said, incensed at the man's callous disregard for what was happening in today's world. "People are so holy up in here, so self-righteous and judgmental, the un-churched would rather take their chances with the other side. Not because they don't want to believe in God, but because they don't want to walk through your brand of fire and brimstone all up in here to get to Him. We should feel some kind of way about that."

Henderson interrupted anything else Tony had to say. He realized that almost none of those drives were coming in his direction. He ranted and raved but in the end, only the board, the deacons, a handful of members and the Henderson family handed him their flash drives.

Tee and Cathy stood in the center of the aisle and shocked everyone by changing course and placing their flash drives in Tony's hand.

"What?!!" Terrance shrieked, his face contorted with rage. "You're breaking rank like that?"

"Enough," Cathy said, pivoting to face her brother. "You're not going to get everything you want, Terrance. Deal with it."

Cathy's brother, cousins, and mother came forward. "You don't go against family, Cat."

"You do when they're wrong," Tee shot back, and her voice was strong and sure. "Pastor Kimbrough's trying to do good here. If they'd had that teen program here, like the one he's thinking of doing in his new church, I probably would be away in college right now. Instead of taking care of two kids, grieving about Najee, and struggling, trying to make ends meet before I'm meeting the ends." Tee shifted her gaze to Tony and Kari. "They've got something good going and I want to be all up in that." She looked at her uncle, then to Aunt Aridell. "You're not going to do anything like they're trying to do. You'll talk a good game and then you'll leave like you always do. You did it before."

"You don't know what you're talking about," Henderson growled, bearing down on his niece.

"She's talking about your first wife and kids," a cinnamon-skinned beauty said from the middle aisle.

"First wife?!" Terrance's current wife shrieked from an aisle over, thrusting one of the silver trays she held in the hands of Sister Carolyn standing to her right.

"Oh, you thought you were the only one?" Aridell chimed in, trying not to smile—and failing as not two, but three more women stepped into the aisle. "Try three. Eight kids. Alimony up the yen yang."

Tony gave her a look to silence her. She was supposed to remain that way during the entire process. Especially when they'd had a little come to Jesus meeting an hour before they walked through the doors to the church.

"Sister Aridell, I'm going to need you to lay off the name-calling," he had said. "I'm going to need you to be a little more Christ-like when it comes to your nephew."

"I am," she replied and had the presence to look a little chagrined. "You'd better be glad I met Jesus and left those F-Words somewhere else."

Tony closed his eyes, pressed his lips together and tried not to laugh. But failed. "Sister Aridell. I'm going to need you to *try*."

"All right," she mumbled, lowering her gaze to the ground. "Can't help it if the man lost a little air during birth and it caused a major malfunction in his brain."

"Sister—"

"I didn't call him a name," she protested, holding up her hands in mock surrender.

Gratefully, she had managed to keep her mouth shut all this time, but from the looks of things, she had pulled off a major upset by inviting all of Henderson's women—known and unknown—to be in the same place at the same time.

"You never told me about any ex-wives or children!" the "new" first lady said, bearing down on Henderson and giving him a shove that took him off balance and landed him on the carpet. "You lied to me?"

"It wasn't lying," he defended, righting himself and his clothes. "I just didn't tell you everything."

"That's lying, especially when you were all up in my business," she shot back. Her fist was at her side, but it was trembling from a need to land in Henderson's face. "Wanted details about my past. Even shamed me about it."

Tee clicked a few keys on her cell, and turned the screen to show the image of a beautiful baby boy. "This one's about a year old."

The wife's head whipped around so fast, it nearly left the rest of her body. "While we were married?!"

"I told her to get rid of it," he protested, quickly looking over his shoulder, eyeing the dubious expressions of the board and the deacons who suddenly didn't seem so pleased with him. "I can't help that she refused. And I don't know if it's even mine."

"That wouldn't be an issue if you could keep that puny little thing of yours where it belongs. Either in your pants or in your wife!"

"Whooop," one of the choir members chirped and almost dropped the box in her hands.

"Which wife," a woman asked from the back of the church. She stood and sauntered up the aisle, a sly smile on her red lips. "Seems like he's confused the current one with the ex. I see him every Friday night."

"Sit down," he growled, waving frantically for Lily to take a seat or shut her mouth. It was hard to tell which.

"And I see him on Mondays. Sometimes Saturday mornings," another woman said, her streaked auburn curls shaking with the effort to effect a sexy pose.

Tony's gaze narrowed on Sister Aridell, who had the nerve to look sheepish—but only a little. Evidently, she didn't wait for Henderson's skeletons to come out on their own. She'd given them a shove and booted them from the closet they'd been hiding in all this time. Now they were rattling up the aisle, bones creaking under the weight of sins Henderson certainly wished had remained unspoken.

He didn't miss the subtle head nod exchange between Tee and Sister Aridell.

"If you haven't told me that, what else have you lied about?" the first lady said, chest heaving with her efforts to remain calm.

"We don't have to watch the *Haves and the Have Nots* anymore," Sister Vera said loud enough for everyone to hear. "Church has been straight drama for the past week."

Several people voiced their agreement with that statement.

The three-ring circus of Henderson exes and currents blocked Henderson's path and were giving him enough issues to keep him busy. A couple of them let loose with a few profanity-laced diatribes and had to be forcefully escorted from the sanctuary.

While Henderson dealt with the unraveling of his personal life, several members came up to Tony and Kari to ask about their new ministry, to which he answered, "We're only in the planning stages right now. We'll let you know."

Henderson's fist shook in the air, but he was smart enough to keep some distance as he said to Tony, "This isn't over."

Tony passed a ring full of keys to one of the board members. "Aside from the counseling records that some of you returned to me today, I no longer have any church records, keys or copies. My name's been taken off all of the accounts." He held up a stack of papers. "Here's a complete accounting of where things stand."

Tony held up another stack of papers. "And we made copies for everyone. It's also on their drives." He leaned in to make eye contact with Henderson. "Now let's see you put in some work for a change."

Chapter 17

Three months later

Henderson hadn't fared well on any level—personally or with the church he'd managed to commandeer. On his first Sunday as the new pastor, only twenty people besides his deacons and board showed up to church. The Sunday after, only ten people came.

Then the deacons and board members found out that Henderson had tried to take out a loan against the building and leave the church with a debt it hadn't been under since Tony took the helm. They had no choice but to step down and turn the church building along with its operations over to Tony. Meanwhile, Henderson's divorce was underway, and his wife was making every attempt to strip him of what little he owned.

As Kari now sat in the pulpit of Temple for All People, she watched people move to their seats to hear her speak. The reporter who had come to her for an exclusive stood in the back, her face pure cosmetic perfection. She had chronicled the Temple's progress in weekly television news segments that showed the hard-working members and the systems they were putting in place.

The teen program had especially been controversial. "Abstinence alone isn't working," Kari had told the mothers, guardians and grandparents at the first meeting. "How many of you waited until you were married to have sex?"

Several hands had gone up.

"I mean for their *first* time."

Those hands lowered.

"'Abstinence only' didn't work for you," she explained. "And let's be honest, it didn't work for a lot of your grandparents or great grandparents either. Yet we're trying to hold today's children to a higher standard when we couldn't do it ourselves." Kari swept a gaze across the women who had varying expressions of shock, anger, and acceptance. "Your teenagers will tell us that they promise to stay virgins, but when those hormones kick in, we're going to end up with more teens with big bellies than we can handle. Today's children need a realistic approach because they're being hit with sexual content from everywhere—radio, television, peer pressure." Then she smiled to lighten the tension in the room. "And they might live under your roof, but when little 'Quan' starts whispering the right things at the right time, they'll forget every rule you've put in place, every threat you've ever laid or every promise they've ever made." Kari tilted her head. "Ask me how I know."

When a clip of that hit the Internet and social media, it went viral. Soon letters, Facebook posts, and Twitter feeds were taking Kari to task for what she'd said. The opposition and support ran half and half, but it didn't faze her either way. The only people she cared about were the teens, who needed a dose of understanding and guidance, tempered with today's reality.

First a trickle of people came to the Temple, then even more. Soon people poured through the doors every week. Most of them people who stopped going to church so long ago that they didn't think God even remembered their names. People who had been hit by life from all sides and didn't believe there was such a thing as redemption.

Oh, but there was. Some of the liveliest conversations Kari and Tony had at the dinner table were those discussions that had to do with Bible misinterpretations. And with every one of them, there was open and honest dialogue, with no judgments.

Kari became stronger each day. After she came out from the darkness and shared her story, Tony had been a ray of light in her world. Now, she was able to help others who were emotionally damaged, and spiritually worn.

It was definitely their time in the sun.

Tony, on the other hand was getting a lot of heat for splitting the ministry into four segments—women, children, teens and men.

Since the Temple was a ministry whose focus was being a support system for women and children who'd survived traumatic circumstances, Tony's first concern was to always make the Temple a safe haven for them. All were welcome, even men with a past. But Tony understood that not everyone who walked through the Temple doors was there to get closer to God. He had frank, private discussions with each man who had a history of sexual abuse or violence toward women and children.

One-third of the men left. Some felt that having the women and children separate from the men was not to their liking. Others refused counseling because they felt that God would accept them as they were, so Tony should too.

"If they were truly here to find God, they wouldn't be disturbed by not having women and children nearby," Tony told everyone. "And women who're focused on getting their lives right won't be all that upset that there are no men here to try and impress. We'll have events and social settings where the groups come together, but this place will be a safe place first and foremost."

Tony stood his ground. And for that, she was grateful.

Now Kari rose from her seat and stood at the podium in the gathering center of the Temple for All People.

"This man right here, my husband," she said, glancing at Tony. "The man I love with my whole heart, has had to have enough salvation for the both of us."

She opened up about her non-belief and the things he'd shared to show her how that one-on-one relationship with God is what was most important. Not religion. Not denomination. Not doctrine. Not a set way dictated by anyone else.

Kari looked away from the audience to lock gazes with her husband, who held up two fingers. Lately, he had been secretive about some "special project" he'd been working on. Every time Kari asked him, he'd simply kiss her and say that she'd know when it was time. She only hoped that time was soon. Though she never thought she'd be suspicious when it came to him, it was getting close. But for now, she pushed all concerns aside, smiled at him, held up seven fingers then took a breath and said in the microphone, "I was fourteen, a freshman in high school ..."

An hour later, Kari looked out at the group applauding after she had shared her story.

From out of nowhere, a young woman ran forward and snatched Kari from her thoughts as she latched onto Kari so hard that she nearly knocked the breath out of her.

"I thought I'd never see you again," the woman said in a wavering voice.

Kari focused on Tony, whose eyebrow shot up and who quickly headed in her direction. She gave a gentle push to allow some space between her and this stranger. The reporter and the cameras moved closer, sensing another story unfolding. Kari held up her hand to halt Tony's movements and the media as well.

"Honey, I don't know who you—"

Those eyes. She *knew* those eyes.

The face surrounding them had filled out to become a beautiful young woman with a heart-shaped face and buttercream skin. But Kari would never forget those eyes. The eyes that once belonged to a little girl who looked to Kari to explain the unexplainable. To help quell the soul-piercing fear that was the constant companion of any female who walked through the doors of Daddy's house.

"I never knew your name," Kari said, microphones from the news cameras picking up every word.

A woman who had stood at a respectable distance came closer, placed a hand on the woman holding on to Kari. "Her name's Jaycee, and I'm her mother."

Kari nodded, noticing that the two women's facial structure was so similar; the older one had no need to identify herself.

"I left her with a family member who let that man take my baby as a payment for a debt her boyfriend owed. They told the police that she'd been kidnapped when they went to the store" She took her tear-filled dark brown eyes off of her daughter and locked them on Kari. "You saved her life."

"No, I—"

"You. Saved. Her. Life," she repeated in a more forceful tone.

Kari sighed, held onto the woman, allowing the joy of knowing the little girl she'd once known in that house of horrors was now safe and healthy. If only the others had been so lucky.

"I'm chasing my master's degree now," Jaycee said, smiling. "Going to be a social worker."

"That sounds real good," Kari said, cupping the younger woman's face in her hands and resisting the urge to embrace her all over again.

"Would you like to go for a coffee sometime?" she asked, her expression hopeful. "Maybe lunch? Dinner?"

"I'd love that," Kari replied.

Jaycee glanced at the cameras and said to Kari, "I would never have found you if I hadn't seen you on the news with your husband when they locked him out of the church. Loved it when he basically told them to shove it." She leaned in to whisper. "But in a Christian kind of way."

That caused Kari to laugh.

Jaycee nodded in a direction away from the press and Kari led the way over to a quieter area of the room, holding up a hand to keep the press and everyone else back.

"I wonder what happened to all the others," Jaycee said, her voice now as feeble as the terrified little girl Kari first encountered.

"I don't know. I only hope they've found some type of peace." Kari took in the tears glazing Jaycee's eyes and said, "Let's not talk about this anymore right now."

Jaycee's gaze shifted to Tony. "That's your husband."

"Yes." Kari beckoned him forward and he closed the distance in a few strides. "Tony, this is Jaycee. Jaycee, Tony."

The three of them walked toward a wall that displayed images of the smiling faces of people in various stages of giving or enjoying one of the Temple's services. "I want to be a part of whatever you're doing," Jaycee said. "I don't go to church. Haven't set foot in one, and didn't think I ever would. I'm still angry with God sometimes. I mean, how could he put men like Daddy out there?"

Kari placed a calming hand on Jaycee's shoulder. "We have a lot to talk about. I asked that same question all the time." She looked to Tony. "My husband is helping me sort out some of the answers."

A woman with soft brown eyes, shoulder-length hair that was more salt than pepper and somewhat recognizable features walked in, scanning the area. She seemed to sigh with relief when she laid eyes on Tony, who left Kari's side and hurried to meet the woman. Together they looped their way through the crowd of people until they made it directly in the space in front of Kari.

For a moment the world stopped and there was no way for Kari to inhale. A tear flowed down the woman's face, followed by another, then more as she stretched her arms out in hopes of an embrace that she didn't appear sure she'd receive.

Finally, Kari was able to move forward and voice one word …

"Mama?"

This was the "special project" he'd been so secretive about? Kari's heart could barely contain all her emotions.

Tony moved back so he was flush with Sister Aridell, who had walked up to join them.

"Why do you always do that—the finger-thing," she asked, keeping an eye on the reunion between Kari and her mother. "She holds up seven, you hold up two."

Tony took his eyes off the two women and put his focus on Aridell.

"The day Kari came back into the restaurant, she said she only needed a six piece, but she walked out with me too."

"Okay, that's seven," Aridell reasoned with a sideways glance at him.

"My two mean that all I've needed in my life is God and her." Tony glanced at Kari, who held up five fingers on one hand, then three on the other.

"Wait a minute," Aridell said, narrowing a gaze on Tony, then looking back at Kari. "Isn't that ... *eight*?"

"Yes. Yes it is," he replied, smiling as he watched Kari's lips form the words, "I believe."

My Time in the Sun
The Naleighna Kai Memoirs

I hope you enjoyed my novella, *My Time in the Sun*. It was a labor of love, written and prepared over a three week period so I could keep my promise of having a new book at the Cavalcade of Authors event in Chicago. I deliberately did not use the name or denomination of a church. I didn't want anyone's focus on the wrong thing. This church could be anyone's church--the one you grew up in or the one you attend right now. At a later time, I'll expand it into a full length novel, but for now, I truly felt inspired to write this and it's in a genre that I've never written in before.

This second part of this book is an inspirational component that contains the family situations and real life experiences that I hope will help be helpful in some way. This is the first time that I've done something along the lines of a memoir, and maybe you'll gain something from reading my words and wading through my experiences.

Straight from the Gate

I was raised by two women who were together for over thirty years. Strangely enough, my biological mother gave me away at birth. She signed into the hospital as her sister, Rose, and dropped me into her arms and didn't look back.

Until fate gave her no other choice.

My "new" mother raised me for eighteen months, then made an unfortunate mistake that earned her a trip to prison. What a family, right? I landed back at the one place my biological mother never wanted me to be—her home. To make matters worse, I ended up with a medical emergency that put me in the hospital for weeks. My biological mother had to take legal steps to ensure I received medical care. She had no choice but to go before the judge, tell the truth about what she'd done when I was first born. The result? My biological mother was forced to adopt me.

But here is where things became interesting. She had taken on a female lover at the time. When I first came to the apartment in the Robert Taylor Homes, a project on the South Side of Chicago, I was told that I went directly to my mother's lover, crawled into her lap and went to sleep. That woman became my "true mother".

My biological mother had been through a great deal, and the way I was conceived added insult to life's already plentiful set of injuries. She was bitter, angered at having to raise the very child she wanted nothing to do with. At one time, in writing a novel, titled *She Touched My Soul*, and giving the character a little of my background and her experience with her mother, I told God that if a certain set of things happened to her which made her hate me so much, then I would be able to forgive her. I let me true mother read the manuscript and she said, "Who told you?" No one had told me a thing. It was all fiction, right? Unknown to me at the time, some of the scenes I created in the novel actually happened in real life. So I had no choice but to keep my word and work on doing what it took to forgive my mother.

Evidently, there were some life lessons I was supposed to learn from the entire scenario, because as you can imagine the physical and emotional abuse was substantial. The only thing that came between us was my true mother, who stayed in their emotionally abusive relationship far longer than was practical. All because she felt the need to protect me.

Once, she did try to leave, but was immediately compelled to return because I had endured a horrific ordeal at the hands of my other parent. That was the summer I left and first ran to my aunt, my "first" mother/ aunt who had served her sentence and was back in Chicago. I overheard a conversation taking place between my aunt and her brother making an arrangement for him to come to her house every week to have sex with me. Something that I wrote about in *Was it Good For You Too?* I didn't stick around to find out the end result, I fled to what I thought was the safety of my father's home.

Unfortunately, that didn't go well.

Overall, when I returned to my childhood home, my true mother was there and I didn't tell what happened at my father's house. I had the common sense to know that she would've ended up in jail. I think she had some idea, but it was nowhere near a normal imagination would take anyone. What my true mother did was to take measures to ensure that I was safe from my biological mother. What she did was to make sure that I would not shut down as a person, as a female, as a human being. She did things to make sure that I would be able to navigate life's challenges without being consumed by any of the negative filters that overshadowed my life. There is more, but I chose to put it in fiction. There's a splinter of my soul and the soul of the females of my family line in every novel that I've ever written:

She Touched My Soul is my healing story.

The Pleasure's All Mine is about my background and my family drama and my relationship with my son

Rich Woman's Fetish has snippets of my sister's experience

Was it Good For You Too? Covers that unfortunate night I overheard that conversation between my mother's sister and brother.

Slaves of Heaven has a great deal of what I experienced by my uncle's hand

Open Door Marriage is a nod to the older woman/younger man relationship with the first man I've ever loved

My Time in the Sun is a blend of my sister and my niece's experiences, with my struggles with believing in God, the recent family drama surrounding a funeral I didn't know anything about, and the tribute to the same man who is written of in *Open Door Marriage, Rich Woman's Fetish*, and *Slaves of Heaven*. Same love. Different experiences.

Now let's take stock of things. That woman, who I call my true mother, was already put in place to help me long before I crossed the threshold and crawled in her lap. I am more like her in my thinking, the way I keep house, and the way that I'm always open and receptive to the beauty of what life has to show me. The Creator knew that I had to go through the tough lessons, but also knew that there had to be a softer, nurturing element nearby to balance things out so that I could become the person, the woman that I am; the woman that I am evolving into. The woman that I am learning to love.

Who knew that things could look really bad in the beginning; but are all part of the Master Game Plan. If things came without walking that thin line between pain and pleasure, fire and ice, seeming failure and resounding success—we wouldn't become the spiritual representation of the best The Creator has to offer.

Ask me how I know.

Six, No Trump

I love my nephew. Let me say that again. I love my nephew. Since the first eighteen months when we reconnected, I have learned a great deal from him. DeMarco was thirty-six then, and the last time we'd spoken to or seen him was at age twelve. Before my son left for school in South Carolina, we located my nephew by finding his grandparent's house on the Southeast side. It was a wonderful day for all of us.

On another note, connecting with him helped with something else. I had always wanted to play Bid Whist. The card game seemed like the "grown up" thing to do. My family was a Spades game family, but on those trips we took down South to Canton, Mississippi with the church, that's when I witnessed Bid Whist players in action. Learning before then proved a bit challenging because some players were too competitive, too serious, and much too impatient. Could almost make folks lose their religion.

My nephew is a champion Bid Whist player; and one thing in particular is the reason he reached that status. When DeMarco sits at a table he *expects* to win each and every time. It's in his walk, "trash" talk, and his demeanor. Ninety percent of the time when he plays, he *does* win.

Susan Peters, one of my literary clients, hosted a party at her home. Sure enough, there came a call for people who could play Bid Whist. I reluctantly raised my hand, but immediately put them on notice that I was a "rookie." There were a few groans as expected; but there was no one else to play with them to make it a foursome—two players against another two.

My partner and I—*clowned*. Boston no-trump; Boston from the low end; Boston from the high end. For those of you who don't play the game, suffice it to say that those are great things. It's when a team has all of the cards/books and the opposing team has none. Soon the game went so sour that our opponents tossed the cards on the table and didn't want to play anymore. One of them glared at me as he left the table and said, "She lied to us. She ain't no damn rookie."

That right there put me on notice. When I told them that it was to lower their expectations of what I would be able to do. In other words, I had already set myself up for failure before even playing the game.

All last year, was about learning to play from the best and with the best. For some reason, it never crossed my mind that I had absorbed the strategies and habits of people who had played the cream of the crop for years. So telling others and myself that I was "rookie" was a far from the truth as I could get.

Lesson learned.

No matter your life's circumstances, try to continuously surround yourself with loving, caring people—people who are about something; people who want more out of life than just working a nine-to-five, collecting a check, retiring and then moseying off into the sunset. I mean, where's the fun in that?

Like me, you came out of the gate with a winning edge—knowing that doing regular things, the regular way is not your calling. Knowing that throwing in your cards because the ones you were dealt don't seem quite fair—is not the way to go. So when it comes to applying this same knowledge to all aspects of your life; you might not want to tell anyone you're a rookie at anything; especially when you've already set yourself up to be a champion at everything.

Blessing in Disguise

All right, I'm going to be honest. I never wanted children. Considering what I had been through early in life, I didn't think there was a maternal bone in my body. So what happened to me at age eighteen? Right at the point I was about to put a "for sale" sign on one thigh and an "open for business" sign on the other? You guessed it, that star in the east floated by; along with Three Wise Men (or was it Three Blind Mice?).

In either case, I was now expecting the one thing I didn't believe I could handle. How was I going to raise a child—a *man* child—without infecting him with the aftermath of my traumatic experiences? Why would The Creator do such a thing? Were they passing the peace pipe up there in Heaven? Maybe someone had three pulls too many. It's supposed to be puff, puff, pass people. At least that's what they said on the movie "Friday".

On the whole, handling the basics: breastfeeding, diapers, shelter, and all that would be easy. What I worried about was the emotional aspects of his upbringing. Was I mentally and spiritually equipped to navigate him safely through to maturity. Especially since his father—a Latino male who was eight years older than my seventeen years—had decided that being a father was not part of his plans. I should've guessed something was a little off about him when he asked me out on a date while my head was half-covered in hair relaxer. But I digress.

My son arrived and he was absolutely beautiful. Politically incorrect translation: he looked like he'd been through hell. He had purple lips and slanted eyes, which made me swear up and down they were passing off the wrong child. Maybe they needed to place him back in the oven and put him on broil for a few minutes. Thankfully, he soon fleshed out and became a little bundle of joy. And that's truth.

Motherhood was especially rewarding. Here was someone who depended on me for everything. A little person who seemed to live for my smiles, my hugs, my voice. A person who needed my protection. A person who I would keep safe at all costs. A person who would inspire me to take risks that I would not have dared on my own. That smile, that voice, that face—that sweetness in his soul that was so unlike me and his father.

My son had such a wonderful disposition that people wanted to give everything, because he asked for nothing. He was never materialistic and that made people do more for him than he realized. For his birthday, he wanted friends and family over—it was never about presents. He did not like to disappoint people. All I had to do was raise my voice and he was sorry for what he'd done wrong. He only needed a spanking once a year, about a month before his birthday when he would lose his mind and I needed to help him get it back. (Yes, I spanked him. That didn't become a "bad" thing until he was an adult).

The Creator knew to pair me up with the perfect child to facilitate a series of lessons of loving someone outside of myself. The lesson of realizing that there were more important things in life than the darkness that I'd experienced growing up. And on another not, the same holds true for my son. He needed to come through his father and me because he had his own series of lessons to learn.

Sometimes the thing that we think we don't want is the very thing that we need for our spiritual development. We'll swear up and down that we'll never do X, Y, or Z. And The Creator says, "Oh, yeah? Let me see what we can do about that." Basically, it's because energy follows thought. When you put emphasis on what you *don't* want, it's taking the focus off the things you *do* want. And trust me, the things you don't want always come with a calling card: Remember that statement you made a kabillion years ago? Well, since you feel so strongly about it, you must really want to tackle it. And then ... BAM! Suddenly you're paddling upstream without a boat, or without a paddle for that matter. You're now tackling a challenge that you swore you never wanted to wade through in the first place.

This is also why it's important not to put anything negative behind the words I Am. Such as I am *broke* (then start wondering why more money's always going out and a lot less is coming in.) I Am sick and tired of being sick and tired. (Have you ever noticed that people who say that always tend to stay sick *and* tired? Or people who are always complaining about one thing or another, always have something new to complain about—every single time you see them?).

Why not refocus your energy into saying: I Am experiencing an overabundance of energy. I Am provided with everything I need. I Am always guided, guarded, and protected. I Am experiencing prosperity in all areas of my life.

I try to start each morning by saying, "I Am grateful for excellent health and strength. I Am grateful for peace of mind and prosperity. I Am grateful for all things great and small." Then I go into the individual people and things that I am grateful for. I set the tone for the day and for my life every day with the words I speak each morning.

What have you been speaking into existence?

Blessing in Disguise - Part 2

With my son, year after year, he never ceased to amaze me. Overall, I thought, "Hey, this motherhood thing isn't so bad after all." I began classes to adopt more children.

Then my son hit puberty and lost his mind on a more permanent basis.

Soon the adoption people were calling me, saying, "Ms. Woodson, you haven't been to classes lately." Frustrated as I was at the time, I promptly replied, "Sweetheart, let me tell you something. I don't want the little mother_ _ _ _ _ I already have, and I don't want your little mother_ _ _ _ _ _ s either."

She asked my son's age and I said, "Twelve." She laughed and asked that I call them back in a few years.

They're still waiting.

Now here's the interesting part. It was a rough time all around and it probably had less to do with my son's antics, some of them life-threatening, than the fact that I had finally found the courage to tell my true mother what had happened to me during those two months I lived with my father.

As I expected, she was ready to end his life. He was taken to the hospital two days later with blood poisoning. No, it wasn't her handiwork or mine, but that timing, though.

Because I was his only known living relative, it took two months of going back and forth to Olympia Fields Hospital before a friend of mine said, "He's waiting for you to forgive him."

In my heart, forgiveness was the last thing he deserved. But I had to give it some thought. My father's condition was such that he couldn't move a muscle; couldn't take in proper food sustenance. He couldn't even blink his lids across eyes that stayed open 24/7. Almost a mirror image of some of the things I experienced under his roof. The doctor let me know that they needed to remove the skin from around his genitals because it was turning blue. I finally gave in, stood by his bedside and said, "Daddy, I forgive you."

I made it home and the hospital had called and left a message. My father had passed away not too long after I left his room.

Now for the reality of things. It took *years* for that statement of forgiveness to become true. Mostly because the real issue was that the person I truly needed to forgive was *myself.* "If only I had stayed and endured my (biological) mother." "If only I had the stomach for what my aunt was setting me up to do." If only … then none of this would have happened.

So at the time my son was having an out-of-body puberty experience, I was having one of my own. That was not the best time for either one of us. But it was my reaction to what was going on with him that made me look even deeper at myself and put me on the initial path of healing.

J.L. was in his own world of pain, wondering what was so wrong with him—a karate, football, and baseball champ—an honor student— that his father didn't love him. Me? I was wondering what was so wrong with me that The Creator would start my life by giving me a ringside seat by the fire next to Satan himself.

Fast forward to December 1999. I began to write about my experiences; weaving them into a fiction format so there was some objectivity. I never understood why I fell into writing; though the "how" was pretty interesting in itself, and something I'll tell at another time.

Soon I started receiving emails from women who had been through similar circumstances. One woman flew in from New Jersey to meet one of the women, a sexual abuse counselor, who was a character in the book. She also needed the type of healing that I had experienced.

That was my purpose. Healing. Overcoming pain/obstacles/ challenges. I didn't know that a novel could help with that. Some women will probably never seek out help. I didn't. My boss at the social service agency where I worked, eventually became my sexual abuse counselor, and later my minister and even more importantly, my best friend. She came into my life when the timing was exactly right. Some women might not ever pick up the types of books that could even point them to a direction to seek counseling or something that would help them to heal. But some picked up *She Touched My Soul,* a fiction novel, and it helped them in some way. My writing also changed the people who were around me. And my life, my inner circle, is filled with people who love me unconditionally.

So, even with all the traumatic and painful things that may have happened, it took some time before I found a way to forgive, heal, and share my truth at every opportunity. One of my mentors, Janine Ingram, author of *Born to be Rich*, mentioned that what's true about God is true about you.

When I needed to learn love, my son was dropped into my womb.

When I finally needed to heal, Sesvalah, my sexual abuse counselor entered my life.

When I needed to learn compassion and understanding, my friend Debra walked in.

When I needed to learn about a God that was unlike the one I knew growing up, Sesvalah, Janine, Janice and Pastor Karen, and Louise Hay became the people who gave the kind of guidance that made a lasting impact.

What my experiences speaks to, is the fact we all carry a vibration that will only attract people who are like us at our innermost core—or the person you are evolving into. That same vibration will carry into all aspects of your life—but it requires recognizing it, applying it, and affirming it on a daily basis.

What are you doing to reclaim your position, your victory over the seeming negative situations in your life? Every day that you open your eyes, take a solid breath, and realize that The Creator has allowed one more day on the journey for you to manifest the very things that you desire.

Have you been speaking "life" into your personal, spiritual, financial, and physical?

Family Secrets

Most of the females in my immediate family have not escaped their share of traumatic experiences.

A thirty-five year old man raped my sister, Eve, in church when she was eight. That set her on a path where at age seventeen, she ran away from home with an ex-con who worked in the lunchroom at her high school, the same one that I would attend years later. That was long before they did background checks.

She would spend years selling herself on the streets, working to get that next high that her pimp provided to keep her working for him. From what I understand, he beat a total of nine children out of her during those years.

When I was ten or eleven, Eve returned home when he had scalded her from neck to lower back. She wore a halter-top on the bus from Memphis to Chicago and had to sit with her face in the forward seat because her skin was exposed all the way down to the pink. My biological mother, and my true mother spent an eternity in Cook County Hospital for her to get treatment. They patched her up, gave her some meds and Eve was on the first thing smoking back to Memphis. Back to him.

Years later, she returned again. Like the time before, she was nothing like the smart, beautiful, curvaceous, girl she'd been before. Time on the streets had put twenty years on her, made her greedy, self-serving and willing to hurt the ones she was supposed to love if it meant getting what she wanted. She tried to flow into a normal life, but the change in her was so profound even I understood that she would never be "normal" again.

Eventually she became pregnant with my niece. My beautiful niece, LaKecia. She was unable to care for her, or the son that came a few years after. Later, after DCFS took both of my sister's children due to neglect, they were placed with my biological mother and true mother. My niece, who we believe had been molested by one of my sister's boyfriends at age give, ran away from home and my mother's strict rules at fourteen and followed in her mother's unfortunate footsteps. Once or twice the police picked her up and she had more than a grand in her pockets from a single night's work.

LaKecia came to live when me when she turned nineteen. By that time, she'd been diagnosed as a manic/depressive and paranoid schizophrenic, possibly triggered by genetics and whatever drugs her pimp was giving her to keep her working. I didn't totally understand the disease/condition, but I learned enough that she improved and started going back to school, and to church with me. She expressed her dreams and goals and made plans to be successful. And when she would laugh and achieve some of the things she planned—the world seemed all right. Hanging with my son helped her a great deal. I guess he'd finally forgiven her for the two times she'd bitten his foot when he was a newborn. (She thought he was a doll). LaKecia's social worker said she had never looked so beautiful and seemed so happy. We only had issues when she tried to skip taking her meds, which is common for that illness. My niece was on the path to becoming whatever she desired.

Then my sister happened.

Though I had put some boundaries in place to protect my niece from herself, I didn't realize she needed to be protected from her mother. There were three rules in my house—finish school, no dating for a while and be home at a reasonable hour. In hindsight, maybe I should have restricted her from contact with her mother.

Eve, who still hadn't healed from her own experiences, promised LaKecia the world in order for her to leave my house and come to hers. Eventually LaKecia fell for those promises believing that being able to do what she wanted and no longer having to live within my boundaries that I put in place was more to her liking. My niece moved back into our childhood home that my sister had "taken over" when my mother passed. It was a match made in hell.

The house was shot at several times one night because my sister owed money to people who weren't interested in waiting for the first or third of the month to get their dollars. Soon, the dealers she owed took over my biological mother's house and everything (and everyone) in it. Including my niece.

Unfortunately, LaKecia was now back in a position that was a far cry from the achievements she'd made in recent months. And there was nothing I could do. Several times I offered to come get her. Even brought the police with me once to make sure that the answers she gave me were of her own accord. Because my niece was an adult, I couldn't force the issue and neither could the officers. That was before things went from bad to worse.

Now she was in a hell of her own making due to choices that were not in her best interest. I am of the mindset that I don't have the bandwidth to fight a battle that someone doesn't want me to win. But I so wanted my niece to be all right. My niece barely survived living in that house and was in and out of mental facilities for a few years. Finally, my true mother had her placed in a facility called Hargrove. LaKecia would come home on the weekends and she stayed with me on a few occasions. She was improving. In the back of my mind, I wanted to save up or bring in the kind of money that would get her the right meds—shots instead of pills that she sometimes refused to take; counseling with the woman who gave me the tools I needed to heal.

Unfortunately, that never happened. LaKecia went into the social worker's office at Hargrove and told him she wanted to go back to school. This man asked her, "Why? You'll never have more than a fourteen year-old mentality."

My niece died two weeks later. Life and death are in the power of the tongue.

While I realize my niece's body had been through some traumatic experiences and she was so very tired; my firm belief is that his statement had dealt her enough of an emotional and mental blow that she was ready to leave this earth. I also was well aware of the issues resulting from the drugs that had ripped through her body, but I would never, never kill the dream of someone who wanted to try.

Trying is growth. Growth is evolving. Evolving is the very thing that we, spiritual beings who are having a human experience, are supposed to do. In my heart of hearts, I believe that LaKecia's desire to strive would have made all the difference in her life. She would rather have rather tried and failed, than be told that she'd never, ever achieve anything worthwhile.

I know the power of The Creator—I know the power of how wonderful life can be when The Creator puts the right people in your path at the right time. It is how I exist the way that I do today—believing that anything and everything is possible. Including overcoming the limitations that others try to put on my life. I'm constantly trying to rise above situations—abuse, molestation, and torture—that put me in the opposite direction of my original start point, long before I even attempted to get out of the gate. Sometimes I equate what happened to me on a Spades or Bid Whist level, when a team goes so far in the "hole" (in the negative on a point scale), that they can't seem to get out again.

My niece had once taken a photo during a shoot for the cover of my novel, *My Time in the Sun*. The picture has a lilac background and my niece is in the foreground draped in a royal purple and gold scarf. The make-up artist had applied hues of lavender to complement her golden skin. She was a princess and was more beautiful than I had ever seen her. My niece's hand was cupped in a pose where the graphic designer was to place an image of her own personal sun. No one could look at that image and tell the hell that she had been through. It is the image of her that I hold in my heart to this day.

That image of LaKecia Janise Woodson is now a reminder that anyone comes to me wanting to do anything, something, to reach their dreams or get to a healing path, I try, to the best of my ability, to help. This image is a reminder of why I write, and why I'm unable to pen novels in a genre everyone thinks I should strictly so I can get an instant book deal or to rake in more money. It's been an experience within itself to be certain I'm not doing too much, or taking over someone else's process, which will stand in the way of that person's life lessons. That will do more harm than good.

When I first typed this chapter a few years ago while at the Essence Festival, I was by the pool, stretched out on the lounger, then I turned over and went back to sleep. I dreamed of LaKecia for the first time in ages. Her image first came through as a baby and she was in my arms. Then a few minutes later, she was a toddler, smiling and laughing and holding onto me. I was crying in the dream because I was so happy to see her.

When I woke, it brought another reality to mind. I still felt guilty and had regrets. If only I had cut my book tour short and used that money to move her in with me again / If only I had forced the police to make her come home with me that day / If only I had loosened those boundaries, then she would have stayed with me instead of going to her mother / If only … then, maybe then, she would still be here on the earth scene.

I think the dream that came to me was for several reasons. She wanted me to know that she was all right. I have forgiven my mother and father who were the ones who put me on an abusive trajectory, but I also need to release the guilt/regret associated with my niece. Guilt and regret are just as powerful as fear, worry, and doubt.

Releasing them has been one of the biggest challenges I faced. At one point, I said to God, you took my mother, my younger brother, and my niece and left my trifling (insert family member's name here), on earth. What reason could you have for that?

Everyone has lessons and a path. Sometimes, though, it is painful to see the ones we love go through the challenges that seem pointless.

In another part of this book, I cover the art of "allowing". This is what helped bring the lesson home.

Jennifer, my number one niece, reconnected with my son and me when she became an adult. She follows a lot of my Facebook posts and there was one where I spoke about "Add on fathers" that sparked a dialogue between us where she was able to get an understanding of who her father, my brother, actually was. The conversation filled in a lot of the "gaps" and "silences" in her mind. I didn't make excuses for him, just gave her the truth as I understood it.

When I came to visit her a couple of months after she had a baby girl, she told me some of the experiences she had during those years where we'd lost touch. She expressed regret about those years, considered them "a waste of time." I was then able to tell her than she shouldn't regret that time or those experiences because Jennifer was stronger than she gave herself credit for. Through her own traumatic experiences, she learned what she didn't want in her life, and it propelled her towards the things that she did.

Jennifer is a wife to a man who waited a long time to be with her, a mother of three beautiful children, and has a career in a medical profession where she excels. What I love about my niece is that she embraces life, and has balance. She has a man in her life that loves her unconditionally—and he makes her happy. That's a bonus. That's what I would want for her most of all.

Once I posted on Facebook, the interesting weekend I had keeping three pre-teens. Anyone who knows me understands that I'm not a "kid" person to begin with, so regaling everyone with some of the things my goddaughter did during that weekend brought some pretty hilarious response. When I posted that she got in trouble, and that I don't spank people's children and then stated that my son was giving me the "side-eye", my niece responded on that post with, "Here's MY side eye." I couldn't help but laugh. She, and her brother, were really good children and I enjoyed having them. I only had to have a come to Jesus meeting with them that one time. She remembers that, but what she mostly remembers was the "cool" aunt who took them to Great America for three days in a row. That's how I did things back them. Took an even number of my nieces, nephews and or their friends, booked two hotel rooms for two nights, and they were able to go to the amusement park from the time it opened until it closed for three whole days. The "cool" aunt was chilling in the hotel right across the street and they were old enough and knew the drill on watching out for each other. She remembers that with so much love.

One of my finest moments with Jennifer is when she told me how much my words have helped her. To me, there is no greater purpose in life, than to help others or to inspire them to a level they never thought possible.

So having the conversation with her about "regrets" provided her some insight from my own experiences. What's in the past cannot be changed. We can only learn and grow from it. We can't go back and rewrite it; take back hurtful words or actions. We can do what we can to right old wrongs, but if the other person is not receptive—move on. Don't let others hold guilt over you and make you "pay" for something the rest of your life. That's not how it works.

One of my greatest joys is helping another person bring a book into fruition. Sometimes part of that is helping the author wade through the darkest parts of their lives and getting them to realize how special they are to have survived the same kind of traumatic experiences I have. That, too, is a part of my purpose.

Have you truly identified what your purpose is? Have you identified that one (or two) thing(s) you would do if you would never see a single dime? Is it making something with your hands? Is it teaching? Is it dancing? Or is it being a life coach? And editor? An author?

Take some time to think about it. But hurry up. The world is waiting for you.

Stop the Train, I Want to Get Off

My son's father, Al, hit a happy milestone several years ago. He made the last child support payment from over a twenty-seven year period. I almost sent him a congratulations card. I had to keep a straight face when my son mentioned that *he* wanted to send him a congrats card for Father's Day. I talked him out of it. I'm sure that dear old dad would not consider it a laughing matter.

I was seventeen when we started dating and he was twenty-five. When I ended up pregnant, somehow he placed the blame entirely on my shoulders. He'd been angry about it for years. So angry that he tried to avoid paying support by taking jobs under the table. Also by taking jobs that happened to be way below his mental capacity. For a time he became a professional student to avoid having a real income. He has blown several good jobs because of it. All this meant is that he could never afford to live on his own. At fifty-eight he's *still* living with his mother. Since his focus was so intent on not doing what a responsible male should have done, he has lived a lot less life than would've been possible if he wasn't so focused on what he didn't want the courts to give me.

Now from his point of view, he might believe that it was my intent to get pregnant. This meant, in his mind, he had every right to be angry. He thought he was dating a mature woman (at seventeen?) who had handled her business, which meant he could have all the fun, but none of the side effects. Good luck that. Especially since he did not consistently use protection. And though I didn't want to get pregnant, I didn't do what it took *not* to get pregnant.

So now I'm about two months along and he has to tell his mother. She had some not so nice things to say about the situation. Even more not so nice things to say about me in her native language. I can understand the N-Word, The B-Word, and the W-Word or its derivatives in any language. I asked him, "Are you going to let her talk about me that way?" To which he replied, "What do you expect me to say? That's my mother." To which I answered, "Looks like you'll be sleeping your Mama from this point on." No, I wasn't Little Miss Sunshine, so I didn't say "sleeping", but I'm trying to keep this p.g.

Now for what was behind door number two. Twenty something years of going back and forth to child support court. Only once in all those years did I need to bring a lawyer to make a court appearance, and that was only because I need to get proper subpoenas for work records when Al finally landed a contract position with the government. Five different lawyers fought on his side that appeared several months at a time and still never managed to get the results he wanted. I went up against every one of them on my own and came out ahead for one major reason. Al pissed off several judges—especially ones who were presented with proof of where every single dime of the child support was going, coupled with visual proof of all of my son's accomplishments.

Once, Al went off the edge and filed a motion to terminate his parental rights to avoid paying child support. The judge told him that he would grant the motion but he would *still* have to pay back child support and until our son reached maturity. Al never mentioned that motion again. Another judge respected my request that Al carry life insurance that was double what he owed in back child support. That meant if he died he would *still* have to pay.

My son was entering his second year at Fisk when I was about to go in for another year of college support, My son said, "Mama stop. I'm going to be married with children and you'll still be going back and forth to court. Stop it. I'll make it on my own."

And he was right. I was going to *make* his father do the right thing. How dare he, a grown man, a man that was older than me starting out of the gate, put everything on me.

Now on his side he was possibly thinking: she's had a house, a car and good jobs. She doesn't need my money. *She* had the child, not me. She could've had an abortion and I wouldn't have this problem.

Truthfully, he didn't see child support as something that paid into the raise his-only-child fund. Funds used to provide the basics, plus karate, baseball, football, basketball, etc. He saw it as, I'm shelling out $$$, not getting any nookie, and this woman is living better than me. What's in it for me? She's the only one who benefits. I never wanted that child any way.

When my son said for me to stop, was when I began to see it from the child's point of view. I was angry before and after every court visit. I was going to *force* this grown man to do what I felt was right. Unlike some mothers, I never used my son as a weapon. Our situation was different; I never kept him from seeing his son. Al didn't want to because he thought process was: I shouldn't have to pay if I'm not spending time with my son. My thoughts were since you're shelling out all that money you *should* spend time with your son.

Same situation. Two different views.

The wheel of child support fortune didn't end until I let it go, forgave him, and forgave myself. The last was the hardest. All those years, I had been resentful of the fact that *he* got me pregnant and then quickly abandoned me; and continuously abandoned his son. He has hurt my son on a number of occasions with false promises of spending time with him, then failing to show—because it was the only way to hurt me. He had been resentful that I got pregnant, and altered his life an continuously made sure I reminded him that he would be paying for one of those many nights we were closer than close.

Same situation, different views. All anger, frustration, resentment, and pain.

The year I took my son's advice, forgave his father and released the whole support thing, was also the same year I received a book deal with Simon & Schuster. The same year I hit the national best sellers list. The same year I received a royalty check that was more than what my son's father took seven years to pay in back support.

I also won't mention that it was the same year my son received a royalty check that covered his school expenses. The same year my son was nominated for an NAACP image award. No, I won't mention it. Because then maybe I might be a little off in my theory of releasing one's deep-seated issues so that the emotional, mental, and financial parts of life will fall in line.

Have things been unfair in your life and seemingly not in your favor? Probably. It's up to you—and only you—to make that change. Who do you need to forgive? What do you need to let go?

Who's in your corner?

In my life, that question has been answered in many different ways
In the beginning of my life: *The Creator, my true mother, my brothers*.

Then it changed to *The Creator, my true mother, my brother, my best friend, my other best friend*.

Then at the beginning of my writing career: *The Creator, my true mother, my biological mother, my son, my brother, my best friend, my other best friend, and my other, other best friend*.

Then at the takeoff of my career with a major publishing house: *The Creator, my son, my best friend; my other, other best friend*.

Notice how the list has changed with every new aspect of my life? It needed to, because not everyone carried the vibration that would work well in the next stages of my spiritual path.

My true mother was my handling all of my money at the start of my writing and had access to all of my bank accounts, all of my credit cards and charge cards—everything. She went into a relationship with a woman that I'd know for years. Surprisingly, they had so much in common and hit it off and soon my true she wanted to wine and dine her; seduce her. The fortunate thing was that the seducing thing she could do on her own. Mama's got skills.

The unfortunate thing was that the wining and dining happened on money she didn't have as she was on a very limited, fixed income. I would totally pay off a business credit card every month and the balance would creep back up without my having purchased a single thing.

When I finally looked into it, I was heartbroken—but I understood. For the first time in almost thirty years. My true mother was in love again. Love can make you do foolish things. But you can't do foolish things that can alter the path of someone else's life. Especially the life of someone who has a goal that will benefit the entire family.

Several other things happened during that time. My best friend, who had moved here to Chicago to escape an abusive husband, purposely deleted an email from a woman who was Stephen King's agent at the time, and requested to take a look at both of the books I had written. I only found out because my son, J. L., installed some type of software on the computer and it accidentally restored all of the deleted emails and made them visible again in the inbox. When confronted, I learned that my friend was afraid that if I became too successful, then she would somehow lose me as a friend.

She did lose me. Trust and loyalty are very important to me.

Then my biological mother died during that time, and she left the money to my siblings—which wasn't a bad thing. But she left the *responsibility* of her final arrangements to my brother. We almost didn't get her buried because he was listening to my sister (yes, *that* sister. They have the same mother and father, but we only share the same mother). They both believed that the insurance and pension money was for them and wanted me to pay for the funeral when there was more than enough insurance to cover everything for her final resting. Then days before the funeral, I stopped answering their calls. My sister's husband started stalking my home in Burnham, a suburb of Chicago. Definitely several miles from where they stayed. That's when I realized that there needed to be a change in my life and my location. I wrote about all of this in *The Pleasure's All Mine*.

I packed up what I could carry for myself and my son, J. L., and left the house that I had purchased for me, my son, my true mother, and my nephew Eric (her grandson) to live together. I turned everything over to the people under my roof—my mother, her grandson, her new lover, and my friend who had tried to derail my literary career. They could all work it out on their own.

I lived in hiding in the heart of an impoverished neighborhood for an entire year. Sometimes, J. L. and I would sleep on the floor to avoid the nightly gunshots. Finally one night I said, "No more. We're sleeping in our beds. If there's a bullet with our names on it, it'll meet us wherever I we are."

My son was the one to move me out of that place before he went off to Fisk University because he didn't want to worry about me. That was one of the best things he could have ever done. And how he, a seventeen-year old pulled it off is another story that's told in his own book.

So I moved on up to the east side, to a deluxe apartment on the corner of 67th & Oglesby with Lake Michigan and Downtown views. The living area had changed, but I continued writing and healing. Then there came a point where I wanted to write stronger male characters.

The first one in *More Than Enough* was a man who only became stronger when two women put him through a male training program because they wanted to share him. The next, *She Touched My Soul*, was a man who was spiraling into drugs before a mysterious woman entered his life and started him on a different path. Then with *Every Woman Needs a Wife*, the male was unfaithful and it was all about him changing his ways to win his wife back.

From that point, I wanted to write stronger Black Alpha Male characters as my lead. My thoughts were that we have enough of the other kind floating around. So I refuse to put them in print unless they are supporting or walk-on characters, but never the lead. Interesting enough, at thirty-nine, I personally didn't have enough to draw on to actually write a strong Black Alpha male.

The Creator solved that problem for me in a miraculous way.

I had always thought that the most beautiful words a woman could hear from a mate was, "I love you." No, not so much. How about the words: "I never knew what peace was until I met you."

Sweet Lord, that's an orgasm waiting to happen.

People say "I love you" all the time, and most haven't given any real thought to what it truly means to love unconditionally. That means it isn't conditioned on the other person doing what you expect; it isn't even conditioned on them returning that love.

But those ten words will resonate with me for the rest of my life. Along with the lessons I learned by being with him.

Those lessons were so profound that I realize he was only in my life for that short time to prepare me for the "real thing." Prepare me so that I wasn't bringing three suitcases, a carry-on, and a trunk instead of a simple tote bag into the next intimate relationship.

The experience prepared me to stop demanding The Creator for things that will slide into my life when it's time. So I don't have a need to say: "I'd like him short, sunburnt, smart, and sensational; tall, tan, tantalizing, and terrific, or butterscotch, sexy, intelligent, and full of fire." Yes, those are all superficial things. I want peace, harmony, joy, adventure, compassion, balance and a host of other wonderful attributes. I want to experience these, no matter what physical form it may come in. I'll let The Creator/Universe handle the details of the when, what, where, who and how.

Another thing I'll share about … Tony. Loving him helped me to love myself more. In my novel *Open Door Marriage*, my lead male, Dallas, and the lead female character is Alicia. Dallas asks Alicia to take a shower with him and she refuses. She is self-conscious about her body, and even more self-conscious about her love for him—a younger man. In the book, Dallas takes matter into his own hands. In real life, the experience was a wake-up call for me.

For two years, I had asked The Creator to send me a man who would love me for me. But the moment that I couldn't step into the shower with him was when I realized that *he* loved me for me, but I didn't love me for me.

Now that I can write about the real thing—I mean love—I can also manifest it. So since my time with him ended in an untimely way, I've focused on having a love affair with myself. I haven't written another list of what I'd like to experience in a relationship. I haven't asked God to send me another mate. No, my wake up call was a startling example of the fact that I need to love me for me. So I've spent time, learning how to do exactly that. And I'm going to be honest; it has not been an easy task. Saying that I love me is easy, showing it is another boat to row. But I'm working on it everyday. And there are people in my corner helping me to achieve success in those areas.

This chapter started with the question ... *Who's in my corner?*

Now to take a look at the kind of corners I have and who's filling them for me at this time.

Spiritual Corner - Sesvalah, Debra, Janice, Janine. Ehryck, J. L., Pastor Karen

Family Corner - my true mother, J. L., Sesvalah, Janice, DeMarco, Jennifer, Debra

Health Corner – Keisha C., *My FB friends who do those challenges with me*

Financial Corner - Debra, Sesvalah, Ehryck, (I should say J. L. since he's hit this corner more often than I would like; but this is all about who contributes *to* the corner—with people who consistently hold my vision of prosperity, or give information/advice that leads to prosperity; or actually contribute dollars.)

Intimate Corner - ***crickets*** But I know he's coming. (I Am being p.g. when I write this—notice the spelling). And truthfully, I haven't asked The Creator to send me another mate because I'm having a love affair with myself.

Notice how there are some people listed in more than one corner? Most times that's the case. People play more than one part in your life. And notice how some people should probably be in more than one corner, but didn't quite make it?

When this is done every four months, it'll be interesting to find that things and people may shift.

Take out a sheet of paper and write down these five corners, then make a list of the people who are in it now. People who have an impact, not ones who are just "holding ground" or "taking up space". These are the people who matter the most. They are the people whose souls agreed to help you with your life lessons when you came to the earth scene.

Next, let's talk about the lightning list (flow of energy—the givers and takers). In your life, there are some people who understand balance. Then there are those who take and take and take and don't even realize you're giving. Then there's also the one-sided relationship where you're the one doing all the work.

There's a little exercise I use to figure out what's what. Why don't you try it for yourself?

Make a circle on another sheet of paper. Write your name in the center.

Then write the names of the people who you interact with most (positive and negative) along the outside of the circle. Now put an arrow from you to those you give your energy to - make the arrow thicker or thinner according to how much energy you give. Now draw another arrow from them to you (thicker or thinner) according to how much energy they give back.

If you're noticing that in some cases the flow of energy is off (not an even exchange); those are the relationships that bear looking into; those are the relationships that need to be shifted or changed—could be your family, children, friends, etc. I'm not saying kick anyone to the curb; but I am stating that affirming a different relationship or a more harmonious and balanced experience might be a good thing.

And as Sean Connery said in the *Untouchables*, "Herein lies the lesson."

Where's The Other Half of You?

One day I walked out of the building where I worked, Frances, one of my co-workers at that time, froze on her way out of the revolving door. She stared at me and her jaw dropped as she asked, "Where's the other half of you?"

Well, what a way to say that.

I smiled and said a simple, "Thanks, Lady."

Yes, she meant the fact that some pounds and inches no longer had a starring role in my life since they'd made an exit stage left. They took their other cast members—lack of discipline, lack of self-worthiness, and lack of self-love—with them for a short vacation. Honestly, they come back from time to time, and I deal with them when they resurface.

But I gave her question more thought. *Where's the other half of me?*

When I first became pregnant with J. L., I was, as I had been since age fourteen, a curvaceous size twelve—built like the proverbial brick house—which attracted the wrong kind of male attention—*adult* male attention. Including my father, my uncle, and the twenty-five year old man who dated me at age seventeen and became the father of my child.

When I first found out I was pregnant, my true mother had left again. She'd had a particularly horrible argument with my biological mother. So I ran away to stay with my uncle and his wife. This is when a family member molested me, for the second time. By the end of pregnancy I was nearly twice the size had been before. By the end of breast-feeding, I was off the charts at two hundred-fifty pounds.

Fast Forward. *Where's the other half of you?*

I thought the most damaging thing that had been done to me was the summer I stayed with my father when I was fourteen. When he made the fortunate mistake of untying me from the portable cot that was my entire existence for several weeks at a time. He was escorting me on one of those infrequent trips to the bathroom. I had enough strength left to bolt for the window, prepared to die so I could finally put an end things.

I broke through the glass, and instead of landing in a crumpled bloody mess on the concrete, actually landed on my feet. The shock of that effort ripped through me as I stood there, amazed that I came out in one piece. No broken bones, only small cuts from the glass. I was totally naked, starved and undernourished, much thinner than when I had arrived, and probably looked a frightful mess. Which would happen if anyone had been through the things I had been through.

Two women, who were having a smoke on the porch, quickly gathered me up. They ushered me inside their apartment before my father put his clothes on and made it down the stairs. They were about to call the police—but I stopped them. My father carried two holstered guns and some type of badge. I wasn't sure what type of agency he worked for, but knew he was great friends with several police officers in that area. I was smart enough to know that they would not be of any help. I asked the women to call the one person who I never thought I would ever want to be in touch with again. My biological mother.

On the way home, I sat in the back of my brother's navy blue Chevy Caprice wearing clothes that the women had given me after they bathed me and tried to get me to talk about what happened. I didn't talk. I didn't cry. I was numb. I was tired. And I was still afraid.

The first words from my mother's mouth were, "Whatever happened to you was good for you."

Yes, she actually said that without knowing what he'd done, or even caring enough to ask. Only later did I understand that she probably *did* know, because he'd done the same thing to her. But her need to always be right, to punish me for embarrassing her by running away again, returned me to the natural order of things with just those few words. Yes, I was home. Back to the same abuse I was used to. An abuse that I could actually welcome after being held up in one of my father's apartments for two months.

Thankfully, my true mother had returned the moment she found out that I was back at the house on Merrion Avenue. She was the one to help me at the beginning stages of healing.

Where's the other half of you? The other *half?* The other half that housed my pain, my sorrow, my guilt, my "what ifs", my anger, my rage, my victimhood, my lost childhood. The other half of me that was weighted down by all of the things that tried to destroy so much in me; the things that took away my ability to trust, to love, to hope, to have joy, to have … peace. *Where's the other half of me?*

I've been releasing those parts of me, working at what is at my core that kept me feeling unsafe—the main reason I feel the weight is/was still on—protection. I could exercise and dance all day long. I could diet and starve myself until the cows walk onto my plate and serve themselves up for dinner. But until I tapped into and dealt with the core reason for why the weight came on in the first place, then it would come back, and keep coming back. Or I would at least have a hard time getting it to come off in the first place.

Dancing might be what I've used as my exercise method; but the weight would not be dropping off as it had if I wasn't doing the spiritual work. Let's be real, though, I've made substantial changes in how and what I eat. But it isn't nearly enough to exact that kind of weight loss that I've experienced. Where's the other half? Seriously? Had I been so disconnected from myself that I didn't realize how others perceived me? Half? At the size I am now? Probably so; and it's probably the same reason that I still don't have any full-length mirrors in my home.

There's a statement that though a person might have been through years of traumatic experience/abuse, it doesn't take those same amount of years for them to heal when it is something they truly want.

Now here's the thing. There are people who are much thinner than I am, who on the outside, appear to be in a healthier frame, but they're holding onto the same types of things that I had been. They might wear it differently—in the form of dis-ease, dis-comfort or seeming illnesses that they manifest according to whatever is going on in their lives. On my part, I can say dis-ease and illness has thankfully not been part of my constitution—no high blood pressure, no joint pain, no back problems, no diabetes (though the count for a long time said I was getting close to pre-diabetic and only a few weeks before the printing of this book, my scale dropped into the nowhere near pre-diabetic range). Weight—the barrier, that wall of flesh has been my manifesting factor. I know exactly when it began, and I know why it's ending. Where's the other half of me? Indeed.

I am finally at a point where I feel safe. And here's how I also know that I have truly created a safe space where I am guarded, guided, and protected at all times. I have surrounded myself with people who make me feel safe and loved. My inner circle—a few immediate family members and a chosen few who are "love" related. These are all part of my safety net; they are the people who reinforce my efforts to heal, to release, to forgive and let go. They are the people cheering me on with every accomplishment; the ones embracing me and dusting me off with any "seeming" missed target of success. The ones who will tell me when I'm out of line.

Where's the other half of me? *Half?* Wow.

Now enough about me. Are you still carrying your other half? I'm not talking about the physical. I'm talking about lack and limitation. I'm talking about pain, frustration, anger, resentment—the kinds of things that result in building a wall around that place within you that is geared and ready to propel you toward success. The kind of things that puts a river between you and prosperity. The kind of things that build a wall around a place in your life where you should have more times of being happy and joyful as well as hopeful and expectant. The kind of things that keep you from evolving into who and what you agreed to be when you came to the earth scene. Because if you don't release those elements, then success will be fleeting; just like weight loss, it won't stay—it won't happen under Grace and in a perfect way—if you don't deal with the core reasons why it's there in the first place.

Some people live their entire lives here on the earth scene buying into the fact that all their lives are supposed to be is about that 9-to-5, marriage, 2.5 kids, the car, the white picket fence, the house, retirement—and that's all folks. But you know differently, don't you? You know there's a greater purpose for your life. You know and feel it all the way down in your soul, or you wouldn't be tested so hard at times. Your challenges wouldn't come in the form of final exams rather than those dippy little pop quizzes or open book tests that everyone else gets. No, you attract the kind of lessons that require an all-day in-class prep, a week of study halls, followed by a fifteen-page essay.

What did you expect? If you wanted to keep your behind in preschool, you'd be lumped in with everyone else—those who are just doing enough to get by; those who are satisfied with small spurts of happiness here and there; small spurts of prosperity that are just enough to cover the bills and take a few vacations here and there. Those who have bought in to the fact that we have to struggle; toil, suffer, and work like the proverbial slave to get what we want. Those who believe that they're a victim of life and they're just rolling with the punches because the punches keep rolling in.

That is so far from the truth.

You have dreams, and goals, and wide-range visions that are far out of the norm, right? So what you've experienced are all master classes and master exams. What you haven't figured out is that now the lessons don't have to hit so hard. You can have them come under Grace and in a perfect way. Does it mean the lessons will stop coming? No. If you glided through life without a few challenges, where's the opportunity for growth?

What this all means is that it's time for you to understand that you can and will have the spiritual umbrella, hip boots, and raincoat to cover you when the "stuff" hits the fan and it's not evenly distributed. That's the way it tends to happen, right? The slings and arrows of outrageous (mis)fortunes seem to miss those who it's supposed to hit and lands right on you. Why? Because it's part of your path, strengthening you for the next set of lessons, the next set of challenges, the next stage of becoming ... you.

Moving on Up

My son stood in the middle of an empty one-bedroom apartment. He glanced around, frowned before telling the property manager, "I'm not impressed." She was a little taken aback by him. J. L. was seventeen at the time. She was showing him the apartment because he made the appointment even after I told him that I couldn't afford to move into that luxury building.

She took him to another apartment. When he was done looking around he said, "I'm *still* not impressed."

Joann escorted him to yet another place.

When he scanned the area; swept through each of the rooms, he smiled at her and said, "*This* is my mother's new apartment."

Now mind you, brother man did not have a job, he was preparing to go off to college in a few weeks, and he was making moves that were waaaay above my pay grade.

I only know the intimate details of what transpired between him and the property manager, because the woman, whose name was JoAnn, called me at work and said, "Your son is amazing." I thought, *well tell me something I don't know.*

But hey, it was her call, and I wasn't sure why she was on the other end of my line in the first place. I had already told her that moving into that building was not going to happen.

JoAnn said, "You know, I have people on the waiting list for this apartment. I have people who have a deposit on this particular apartment; but if you want it, it's yours."

I did a mental sweep of my finances. Deposit, Security, moving costs—and came up snake eyes. When I told her I wasn't moving in, I had immediately paid next month's rent in the spot where I currently lived. So I was on empty.

"JoAnn, I would love the place, but right now it's not looking too good."

"Think about it, then call me back and let me know." This was on Wednesday.

I received another call that evening. One of my former publishing consulting clients wanted me to slide by her house in the morning. Morning? Back then I wasn't a morning person. I wasn't an afternoon person. (As quiet as it's kept, I wasn't an evening person either. But I digress). But this woman wanted me to come to her place before work because she needed to speak with me. So the plan was take a cab to her, then the bus to get to work on time.

I was at her place in Jackson Park Highlands early that morning and it was the fastest meeting in the world. She simply slid an envelope my way and said, "I really appreciate all you've done for me and I just wanted to say thank you."

That envelope contained enough cash for the first month's rent in the new apartment, which was double the rent of the current duplex I lived in. (Baby, you can thank me with Benjamins anytime you see fit.) To say I did the Electric Slide all the way to the bus stop was putting it mildly. I had never charged her a consultant fee for doing her books; and she became my mentor, almost like a fourth mother. One would think I'd have had enough of those already, right?

I called JoAnn when I made it to work and said, "I have some cash in my hot little hands. It's enough for the first month, but I still don't have the security just yet."

"We don't normally do this ..." JoAnn replied.

Don't you *love* when sentences start that way?

"But I'll spread the security over several months," she said. "We'll tack on an additional one-hundred per month until it's paid. You'll sign a separate promise to pay document. How does that sound?"

"Sounds like I'll be taking the apartment. Thank you soooo very much."

"You can move in on Saturday," she said.

"Saturday? But that's two days from now."

Two months before I started claiming a new place, I started packing and getting rid of excess, but I wasn't close to being finished.

"Yes, but it's ready," she said. "And I have some guys who'll help you move if you need them."

Done deal.

On that Sunday prior to the call with Joann, my minister, Sesvalah, the author of *Speak it into Existence*, had talked about "Taking God out of the box."

The same energy you use to ask God for a two-room shack is the same energy that God can use to supply you a mansion. The same energy you use to ask God to supply you with a Hooptie, is the same one He can slide you into a BMW.

Seriously? Where they do that at? It's as simple as speaking it into existence?

The week before, I had already told Joann I wasn't going to be moving in. But I took that message seriously and started thanking The Creator for my new two-bedroom, two-bathroom, deluxe apartment with a balcony, all appliances, and an excellent view of Lake Michigan and Downtown Chicago. I started thanking The Creator that I already had it. But going by my finances there was *no way* that I could have moved into that place. Putting it out there made my angels, ancestors, teachers, and guides move into action, got them off the Bid Whist tournament they were holding in the background, and started them on coordinating things so that my desire could be met.

Even when I felt that it couldn't happen, my son held the vision for me. Held it strong enough that the property manager was moved by his faith and allowed me to have that apartment.

The sermon was on Sunday. I started claiming on Monday. J. L. saw the apartment on Wednesday. I visited Bettye on Thursday morning. I put in the first month's rent, signed the lease and arranged the movers for Saturday on Thursday afternoon. I was in my new two-bedroom, two-bathroom, deluxe apartment with all appliances and Lake Michigan and downtown Chicago views on that very Saturday afternoon.

I won't mention that when I called the place where I lived at the time and mentioned that I was moving out immediately that they requested for me to send them a letter dated for thirty days prior stating that I was moving out. They gave me every single dime of my current rent and my deposit back.

I won't mention that I lost my job two weeks after I moved in. I won't mention that through The Creator's grace and mercy, I never missed making a rent payment in the seven years that I lived there. I won't mention that the only reason that I finally moved from that beautiful place was because the building, after thirty-five years, was sold and the vibration of the building, management and the new people they were moving into it, changed drastically. One of the property managers switched to a new job, and made sure that I slid into the new building she managed. Even gave me a month-to-month lease, all with the understanding that I would be trying to buy a house at some point. No, I won't mention any of that because that would seem like everything was too much of a coincidence.

Oh, but I will mention that there was another reason I was supposed to be in that wonderful space on Olgesby. JoAnn had been trying to write a book for years. I helped her with the beginning stages of getting her book done until circumstances didn't allow us to work on it for a while.

One of her family members contacted me right after JoAnn made her transition. JoAnn's last words to her sisters were, "have Lissa to finish my book." After everything she had done for me, how could I say no? I took on the task of ghostwriting the book, *Thrift Store Junkie*, and keeping it in her voice and with her ultimate concept—that everything, even inanimate objects have energy that can affect those around it. Certain awesome events had happened in her life had been brought on by her love and purchase of second-hand things. Weaving those accounts into fiction was right in my wheelhouse and I truly enjoyed and was grateful for the experience. Her sister presented *Thrift Store Junkie* at my Cavalcade event at the South Shore Cultural Center. The book sold out its first printing.

What happened with JoAnn, J. L. and all of the people involved in this scenario, is all Synchronicity. *Synchronicity is the experience of two or more events as meaningfully related, whereas they are unlikely to be causally related. The subject sees it as a meaningful coincidence, although the events needn't be exactly simultaneous in time.*

The Creator aligning things so that my desires can be met feature prominently in most of my stories and in my life:

How my true mother came into my life

How I needed to learn to love unconditionally and my son was dropped into my life

How I wanted to learn to play Bid Whist and my nephew and his family and friends kicked in

How I asked The Creator for a "placeholder" until the real number comes along, and Tony swept in and out of my life

How I wanted to feel safe, guarded, guided and protected, and several recent incidents have proven this to be the case.

How I asked The Creator for the "real thing" and I'm provided a lesson that showed that I wasn't ready.

Here's your new assignment: I'd like to you to write about some of the times that you recognize that The Creator and synchronicity has been at work in your life. Be mindful of every element, every person and their contribution to your highest good.

Tony

Something happened at work one day that I found pretty interesting. I was handling the travel expenses for one of my wonderful female attorneys and things didn't quite add up. *Hmmm ... two bottles of beer and two glasses of wine at dinner in a body that is much too tiny to soak it all up in that short span of time. No, that's not like my lawyer at all.*

Some legal assistants would have just let it slide and let the accounting people call her on the carpet about charging so many drinks to the firm. Even though I didn't know whether she indulged or not, I knew that much liquor was out of character for her. Now if it had been the partner I worked for, I knew that man could drink me, you, and everyone in the building under the table—no problemo.

I walked into my lady lawyer's office and asked, "Hey, is there any chance you had this dinner with someone else?"

She frowned, then her eyes grew as wide as saucers. "OMG, yes. I certainly didn't have all those drinks myself."

"I kinda thought that," I replied, giving her a smile.

She circled the items that were hers, which didn't include *any* of those four drinks whatsoever. "Thank you for catching that."

To which I replied, "That's what I'm here for. I'll always have your back."

I'll always have your back.

About five years ago, I met someone who I believed was totally out of character for me. I thought The Creator knew me, but a bad boy from the wrong side of the tracks drops into my life the moment I walk into my favorite Jamaican restaurant. Seriously? This is the best The Creator could do? I mean, you've had my back on book deals, tours, getting my son in college, getting me into a wonderful apartment, getting this job— and you want to send me who? Awww, come on.

I'll always have your back.

For two years, I had written my intentions of things I wanted in my life. Everything from prosperity, to book deals, to the right job. When I wrote about a mate, I focused on what I wanted to experience in a relationship—peace, unconditional love, compassion, respect, honor, joy, understanding, excellent communication, etc. I think I had over thirty attributes on that sheet.

Two years passed and nothing happened. Not a single thing. Then I finally got angry and said to The Creator, "All right, if it's going to be a minute, then could you send me a placeholder until the real number comes along?"

I'd said that line in anger, because all my others: new car, hitting the *Essence* bestseller's list, that start of being debt-free and several things had come to pass. But this whole unconditional love thing must have been a Veggie Whopper of a request—because all I heard was "crickets" in that department. *Helloooooo. Are you hearing me up there? Is there an echo in the house?*

So when I added that whole: if it's going to be a minute line … I was pissed off. And The Creator gave me back what I put out. Enough to fulfill my request and shut me up at the same time. And more than enough to prove that I wasn't ready for the very thing I requested. The experience taught me that I needed to *get* ready because the real thing was going to need to meet me at a certain level/place/consciousness. And I certainly wasn't there yet.

Yes, The Creator has a wicked sense of humor.

I'll always have your back.

Now here's this person—a younger man—who is totally out of my element; totally out of character; totally not within my wheelhouse; who steps to the forefront and into that space. Had me asking what the heck did I create in my life? What did I ask for?

But let me tell you, that brother brought me a set of lessons that practically forced me to splinter his soul into four separate books to analyze them, to appreciate them, to recognize what I was supposed to take away from them. I only had three months with him. A placeholder. Three whole months.

I'll always have your back.

I intimidated him—a little. Okay, maybe more than just a little. Mostly because, in his mind, I was up here (hands above my head); and he was struggling to make ends meet without meeting the end. Never knowing what to expect from him because in my mind we had absolutely nothing in common, intimidated me. *Well, at least he isn't one of those sagging pants types.* But the man could wear the hell out of some well-pressed solid T-shirts and jeans. I deserve better than all that, right? A six-figure man or something like that. What did I know?

When Tony would come to the apartment he would stand in the center of the living room, admiring the beauty of it; how clean it was; how neatly everything fit in place; how sparse it was. I'm a minimalist and don't believe in clutter or filling up every bit of space where I live and it showed. The quiet, the peace—sanctuary. *That* was what impressed him more than anything. Only later would I learn that I—just by being myself—was what impressed him most of all.

I think what set him on his spiritual journey was opening to me on the very first night, being vulnerable, sharing his truth—a truth that frightened me at first. *Really Universe? You're going to test me this way?*

I'm going to be honest. He was already working at the place I first saw him—one of my favorite restaurants. But he had that "edge;" that let me know he'd probably been into some other things—things that women like me should stay far away from. I knew that going in, even though I didn't have a single shred of proof.

If I want to be taken for who, what, and where I am; then I had to start by doing the same in all of my relationships—intimate or otherwise. A lot of people go into them with that whole fixer-upper mentality: "When I clean him up, he'll be the perfect man" or "When he gets a real job" or "When he starts making those six figures, he'll be all right with me." When the truth is more along the lines that people are simple "as is" take them or leave them because when you try to "fix them" and it's not part of their path or life's lesson, then it ends up being one hell of an undertaking for everyone involved. Not to mention a whole lot of unnecessary pain and suffering. Ain't nobody got time for that.

But this—who *he* was—was a true test of my mettle.

Here's my take on the situation. Evidently, Tony had put out there in the Universe that he was ready for a change in his life. That request went up about the same time I had let loose with that angry little diatribe about having a placeholder, having unconditional love. People, we have a match made in Hell? Heaven? … well, in *something*. At the time, I wasn't quite sure.

To make matters worse, the chemistry between us was so strong that we couldn't hold a decent conversation unless we sat on opposite corners of a room. No getting around the physical attraction aspect of things. I couldn't run away if I tried. Oh, and I did try. Bottom line? We were supposed to be mated. We were supposed to share time, space, and energy.

So for some reason, we're on the same trajectory. We both have a set of lessons to learn and evidently we're the best two people in male and female form—with the right balance and chemistry—that are suited for the job. What did I ask for again? Oh, right. Unconditional love—from a placeholder.

I'll always have your back.

Tony was a challenge for me out of the gate. I was a challenge for him out of the gate. Mostly because I don't go in for the games that people in relationships tend to play. I'm all up front, lay the cards and your hand on the table, pick it up and run with it, or take your toys and go home. I'm also very clued in to when people try to play games with me. But of course he had to try. That's what he was used to with women. Used to them making concessions for him just so they could hold onto a fine specimen of handsome milk chocolate male that wasn't half-stepping when it came to the things a woman screams about.

So after making that initial connection—dynamic conversations over time, a powerful session of toe-curling, earth-shattering foreplay one night; life-altering, bar-raising love-making several days later—he's at a point where ... "I got this. Yeah, I'm going to see how far I can take her; I'm going to see how I can get into her mind and take it over."

People, I let him roll right over that ego cliff all by his dammy. And didn't even slide him a rope to let him at least hang on for a few minutes before dropping off into the ocean.

In other words, because I didn't immediately give him what he wanted—to move in with me, he threw the typical male tantrum. I didn't hear from him for about a week. Cool. In my mind, it was ... "Well, the "placeholder" must have been all about getting the oil changed, a tune-up, an AC flush, new spark plugs, interior and exterior detailing, and the whole certified pre-owned vehicle overhaul. Fine with me." If that was The Creator's way of teaching me a lesson about throwing requests out there with the wrong sentiment—so be it. Lesson learned. (Oh, but thanks for tightening a sister up in the process. High five, Creator. High five!).

But it wasn't over.

A week later, I received an unexpected call from him. And I could tell it took every ounce of effort for him to find that one humble bone in his body which allowed him to say, "If I let this thing between us go, if I let you go; I know I'll be making the worst mistake of my entire life."

I can appreciate sincerity in any form. I realized it took a lot for him to say just that and sum up his feelings. Did I go into, "Well why you ain't call me"—and add the classic sister neck rock? Did I make him sweat about it? *Well, let me think about and get back to you.* No. What purpose would it serve? I don't play games. You lay it on the line—if I'm open, we're rolling. Try to manipulate me, I'm done, and *you're* rolling. If you come to me as a man, admit your mistake—there's no need for me to ride it into the ground. If I make a mistake, I own up to it. Apology accepted? Alrighty then. Not? I guess this is where I get off the train and let you ride the rest of the way without me.

I never said to him that in order to be with me you have to change—you have to leave that part of your life. I never said that; never implied it either. I accepted him for who he was. Evidently this was something *he* wanted, *he* needed for his soul's evolution. And he, with everything he brought to the table—which was purely himself, was exactly what I needed for my soul's evolution. That made it the perfect opportunity for spiritual growth, no matter what it looked like from the outside or at any angle.

I'll always have your back.

And things were simple. Sharing. Talking. Dreaming. All equal footing and finding common ground, finding balance. Getting his point across to me was simple. "Baby, you know what you just did was illegal, right?"

"What?"

"That turn you made from the far lane and down 79th. You could get pulled over for that."

"Really?"

"Really. From now on, you need to slide up South Chicago, cut through the lot and *then* roll up 79th."

"Okay."

Getting my point across was simple. Once when I prepared to get into the car, I paused for a moment and looked at him and said, "This is the first and last time that I open my car door when I'm with you."

A split second later, he came around to the driver's side and held it open for me as I slipped into the driver's seat, but he asked, "Suppose there's someone shooting at us? I'm supposed to hold it open for you then; when we should be breaking camp?"

I looked him square in the eye, replying, "If there's a bullet with my name on it, it'll catch me standing still. I'm not running. I prefer to meet my fate head on. I just hope they don't miss."

Tony stared at me for the longest time. End of discussion. Point taken.

Amazing that is exactly how he died. A bullet. To the chest. On the night that he had told his people, "Y'all won't see me for a while. I'm going to My Light. I'm going to my Comfort Zone." That is what he called me. *His Light. His Comfort Zone.* He never gave my name to anyone in that part of his life. I was something that he kept all to himself. I was his … sanctuary—the place that he could come when the world was giving him a swift kick in the rubber parts. The place where he could make sense of things that seemed pointless and endless.

The barrier between that part of his life and mine was also the main reason that I didn't find out he'd been killed until the day of his funeral. Correction—*after* his funeral had taken place. Killed by a man who he'd had an angry exchange of words with a few weeks before. A man who was upset about the amount of power Tony wielded even though he wasn't one of the men at the top of the grid. A man who was angry about the changes Tony was now making in his life. Positive changes that some couldn't understand and some didn't appreciate. He was making the change in his life—for himself and it was affecting everyone he knew.

But oh, The Creator wanted me to know that Tony wasn't killed on some bull—because that was the first thing that crossed my mind. The thought that had *stayed* in my mind.

I didn't know it then, but learned the next day after his funeral that the daughter of one of the women of my church was his right hand on that side of the spectrum. They had said she was "rough." I didn't know they meant *that* kind of "rough." When her mother passed me the phone, Kay said, "Lissa, I can't talk to you in front of my mother; but I'ma call you, a'ight? I have to talk to you. It wasn't what you think, a'ight?" How the heck could she know what I was thinking?

Kay called the next night and said, "We *knew* it was a woman. We knew it was a woman!! The kind of changes he was making—only a woman can have that kind of pull on a man. And that's all he was talking about was his Light; somebody he said was his Comfort Zone or something like that. Said that there were better things for us; that we didn't have to have a whole lot of money or education to reach our dreams and goals. We just had to try. We had to put it all down on paper, then get out there and try. No excuses, no b.s'ing, balls to the wall …We could change our lives. We really could.

"You know we were going to _____ (I can't remember the restaurant she said), to celebrate. To put a toast up for what he was about to do.

I found out that he was going to enter into a program that accepted men with his type of past which trained and placed them in higher paying jobs. I had looked up the information for him when he asked, but I didn't know that he had actually went through the process of getting in. He had called me earlier that day and told me he had good news and he was coming to me that night to tell me. He never made it to my place.

"You know," Kay said. "He had us out there on the block—at sometimes, three, four in the morning, writing down our goals and stuff like that. Saying we were all getting out of this. All of us. He was talking to us about changing the way we think and how we look at things."

I think this was the point that I burst into tears. I never knew how much of what I said to him that he actually took in. But to hear that he was trying to get the people around him to understand principles that he had just learned, was a powerful thing to me. That was what love felt like.

I told Kay, "I didn't think he really listened to me. We were only together for a few months."

"Lissa, if you were able to get him to change his life in two months, two days, twenty-four hours or whatever, and that was something nobody else could do in twenty-eight years—then that's what you were about. That's why he was with you."

Well, sum it up for me why dontcha?

"I'm glad that he had a good woman in his life; because he really was a good person at heart."

She gave me several examples to illustrate her point and I had an even greater appreciation for the man I barely knew. Tony was a walking contradiction. But the truth of the matter is that it wasn't about me. It was a change *he* wanted to make. The Creator knew that his soul was about to make that exit; but there were some things he needed to do *before* that happened: 1) a turbo jump from one type of consciousness to another 2) to be an answer to a request I had put out in the Universe 3) to be an inspiration to those that were in that life with him.

Kay took Tony's advice and got out of that life like he'd encouraged her to do. She's now married, has three children and a degree. That was one of the goals and dreams that she wrote down one of the mornings she and Tony were on their "shift."

I believed that The Creator sent me someone who I felt was totally "out of character". But it ended up being the best experience for me. At least to date. He had to have the right blend of everything—strength, experiences, and background included—to provide whatever lessons that I had opened myself up for by laying that request on so thick.

I'll always have your back.

And here it is, I thought The Creator was a little ticked off at me for snapping the way I had. No, the experience was all about showing me that my prayers and requests are always answered even if the answer is, "No" or "Not right now." The experience showed me that I needed to stop thinking that things will come in a way where I have total control or that it will look, taste, touch, smell, and sound a certain way.

The lessons from Tony have echoed with me for all this time. As a "placeholder" it was a starting point for realizing that I needed to release a whole lot more. But more importantly, I needed to love myself more. I needed to love myself *unconditionally* before I could think about forming my lips to speak or poising my fingers to place another tall order of a request to The Creator about having a mate.

I'll always have your back.

Indeed. The Creator sent me Tony as an answer to prayer. I definitely consider that having my back.

Karma Comes With a Calling Card

Karma or Reaping what one sows has played an important part in my life. This part of my story comes with a little bible commentary first. Truthfully, I want you to picture that this is how Pastor Tony Kimbrough of my novel would have his Sunday lessons. Stay with me, there is a purpose. Or skip to the end of the biblical reference and go straight for how I tie it all in.

Do you know my favorite person in the Bible? Yep, you guessed it. David. Why? Because David was honest about his sins; he was a straight-up whore, loved to have a great time, partied like a rock star (and if the way a certain Bible verse reads about the death of his dear friend Jonathan, *"You have been very pleasant to me. Your love to me was more wonderful than the love of women"* he might've been into more than we gave him credit for. (Hey, I did say that he partied like a rock star, right? And you know David loved him some women—a lot of them, so if what Jonathan gave him was better than *that* ….))

What really makes me love David is that no matter how much dirt he did, he loved The Creator, always gave respect where respect was due.

And he still managed to be the apple of God's eye and continued to be blessed—simply by being himself.

So let me get this straight, sleep with everything wearing laces and shoe leather, kill off the husband of the woman that we want to marry; eat, drink (a lot.) and be merry and *still* come out on top? Well, sign me up for the long program. Yes, indeed.

David seemed to always have things go his way. But let's look at things from several perspectives—the very things that took him off his square. David was walking on the roof of his palace as he did every evening, saw Bathsheba talking a bath and in typical kingly male fashion, he said, "I'd like to hit that." On the flipside, we have to think about the fact that people back in those days were modest and walking around naked wasn't exactly the "in" thing. Sooooo, there's a great possibility that Bathsheba timed things correctly, put herself out there on purpose so that she could catch David's eye, seduce him and trade up a husband.

Now mind you, David wasn't short in the female department. He had a slew of wives and concubines already. But he still had Bathsheba summoned to his place and they did the doggone thing. I mean, how could she refuse having sex with the king? And he wasn't bad on the eyes. *And* if his reputation proceeded him he could handle his business and then some …

No problem. Then she got pregnant. *Big* problem.

At the time, Uriah, Bathsheba's husband was off fighting a war for David. So, if hubby wasn't there to do the honors … then who's the baby's daddy? David quickly tried to cover things up by bringing hubby home to hurry up and get it on with Bathsheba. Then the baby could be born under the cover of their marriage bed and David would be off the hook.

Well here's where things became interesting. Hubby didn't do as he was commanded. Instead, he slept inside the wall of the castle with his men rather than go home to his wife. Kind of makes me wonder if that's the reason Bathsheba was so ripe for the plucking in the first place. But I digress. Hubby was actually following an ancient kingdom rule applying to warriors in active service. So he gets a pass.

Several times hubby doesn't follow David's orders that would put him in bed with the wife in enough time for the baby to "officially" be considered the hubby's. So what's a lover to do? A lover with the type of power that David had? He sends Uriah off to war again. This time he makes sure old boy is on the frontline so the enemy will do David's dirty work and kill him off. That sounds like some *Scandal* or *How to Get Away With Murder* type stuff to me. The plan worked and David married Bathsheba and moved her into the palace. Happy times, right?

Even though David was the apple of God's eye and all that, The Creator was not pleased with what he'd done. That was some low-down dirty stuff up in there, up in there. First rule of when you're about to do some dirt, if you can't do it all yourself, then make sure the cast of characters who know everything remain small. David thought he had covered all the bases. Only a few people knew the real deal: a) the messenger he sent to Bathsheba's house to bring her to the palace for a little slap and a lot of tickle, b) the general he used to put Uriah on the front line c) Bathsheba herself.

Here's the thing: The Creator knew and because David was full of himself and wasn't listening to his angels, ancestors, or his own self-accusing spirit, the point had to be brought home in a different way.

The prophet, Nathan, came to David and told him the parable of the rich man who took away the one little ewe lamb of his poor neighbor (II Samuel 12:1-6), and the story made David angry. So Nathan hit him with a zinger by comparing the story he'd just told to what David had done with Uriah and Bathsheba. David was instantly remorseful and confessed his sin. Bathsheba's child by David was struck with a severe illness and died a few days after birth. David accepted that as his punishment.

The Creator had given David so, so much. Had taken him from being a lowly shepherd boy to being a powerful king. And *this* is how you returned all that favor? *This* was what happens when you become top dog? Seriously? No, no, my brother, you won't get off that easy. Let me bring that lesson in a way you will never forget.

Absalom, one of David's sons, was planning to take over David's territory and declare himself as king. What better way to show "who's the man" by having sex with ten of David's women. David slept with *one* woman. His son slept with *ten* of his women. And he did it … drum roll please … in public. Sex with ten women out in the open. (See, I knew those Bible types were getting it in back then). Now you know David wasn't going to take that lying down (no pun intended). This led to a rebellion that plunged the kingdom into war.

Sleeping with Uriah's wife, trying to cover it up, and killing off the husband had repercussions that far outweighed the loss of their child born of a murderous and adulterous liaison. Several lives were lost in that first war, and then in the war that transpired long after. David's kingdom, family and friends were all in an uproar—all the product that stemmed for one incident.

In the beginning of David's life he was more in control of the flow of his life; directing it, following his inner spirit and what The Creator had lined up for him. All good things came his way. After the incident with Uriah and Bathsheba where he let dark consciousness take his life for a test drive, David's family is out of control. His son, Ammon, raped his own half-sister, Tamar, another one of David's daughters, within days after the incident with Bathsheba. Then later Absalom loses his mind and overthrows the Kingdom. All in all, it seems that David is more tossed and turned by the events happening within his life than being in the driver's seat as he once had been. He was reacting to things that happened, rather than taking things in command as he had always done—because he had lost that connection with The Creator.

Though all that had transpired, Bathsheba gave birth to Solomon who would succeed his father to the throne although there was another child next in line after Absalom had been killed. Solomon became known as the world's wisest man and he wasn't half-stepping either. What was he into … like 700 wives and 300 concubines; some of them were his father's. Busy man. Busy man. Both men had their strong points and their flaws; but they equally had the greatest impact on the history that we find in the Bible.

What does all of this tell us? The most powerful outcomes can come from the most interesting of circumstances. But that everything we do, good, great, bad or ugly sets the stage for what comes back to us. If we don't live in our purpose, or listen to that still, small voice or whisper as Oprah calls it, then we're not in the driver's seat. We're letting life happen *to* us instead of letting it happen *for* us. Now you know at some point, that still small voice whispered to David, "You'd better leave that man's woman alone." But his ego answered that little directive with, "But *I'm* the king. I'm running things up in this camp. I can have all the women I want and then some."

Yeah? So how did that work out for him?

So let's talk about Karma for a minute. It's a word that basically means, "you reap what you sow". Whenever most people talk about Karma, they're meaning only the bad things because that's what makes the most impact and stays fresh in the mind. Sometimes we tend to think that people who have done us wrong don't seem to be getting *their* share of Karma, like we're getting ours.

Not so. They do.

Karma. There's the good kind. There's the bad kind. But you know what we remember most? The kind that comes with a calling card that says, "Remember that stuff you did? Well, you placed a full order of payback—and heeeeeeeeeere it is." Then wham! "The stuff" starts rolling downhill, and you're not able to get out of its path before it lays you flat on your back. The minute you try to get up and dust off, them— Wham! Another one hits.

You might ask yourself, "What did I do to deserve this? I'm a good person; I don't do anybody any type of wrong. Why is all this happening to me?"

But the bigger question we ask when we're catching hell and the people we think should be catching it, too, is: "Why do they get off so easy?"

Remember, you're not with that person every waking moment. So you don't know how it hits them. You're not privy to every single thing that's happening in their lives. You only see the surface. You only see it through your pain-stained lens. You can't know a person's inner pain and struggle. They only can see yours because when they flex and inflict pain, you react. Then we start taking notes and comparing. They hurt me; harmed me; but they don't look any worse for wear. The Creator will revisit their efforts in due time and can handle it a lot better than you ever could.

Let's take my father for instance. I could *never* have inflicted the type of pain and suffering he caused me. When he was lying in that hospital bed for more than two months, in pain, couldn't move a muscle, couldn't blink his eyes, his entire body paralyzed from head to toe—but his mind was totally active and aware of everything going around him. I could never have done that. But it happened. And for some reason The Creator knew it needed to happen where I could see it. But it doesn't always work like that.

But here's the kick in the rubber parts; I got no joy out of seeing him that way. Not a single ounce of pleasure seeing him suffer. Why? Because that's not who I am. Reveling in someone else's pain or misfortune is of dark consciousness. It's almost childish in the sense that you want to stick out your tongue and say, "Nah. That's what you get. You shouldn't have done that to me."

That might have felt great when we were children and didn't know any better, but now—really? Is that what we're about? No, I don't think so.

But what that incident showed was that The Creator/Universe always has a better way of taking care of things. Including people who have hurt or harmed me. Because then it is about the other person's lessons, that have been brought on by what they have signed up for and what they've done to others. It's not me getting all up in the mix trying to figure out what I can do to them to pay them back; to inflict as much pain on them as they have on me.

All in all, The Creator takes care of the things that need to be taken care of—you, me, our families, our friends, our enemies, total strangers—everyone. You don't have to see it in order to know that it works. Just believe that it does.

Sounds like a plan?

If You Can Spot It, You've Got It

If you can spot something you don't like in someone else, that means you also have it somewhere in you—even if it's on a small scale. And it's something that might need a little work.

An author brunch in Chicago was held where I was the featured speaker. I had a gazillion books, two assistants (J. L. and my nephew), and Deb, one of my Road Dolls—a woman who has been moral, spiritual, emotional support since the beginning of my writing career. At first the venue coordinator was going to stuff me at some small little card table in the corner. I wasn't feeling it. She was busy accommodating vendors and other authors with what they needed, and wasn't feeling my need for a larger table, the same size as everyone else's, so I wouldn't look like I rolled up in there Beverly Hillbillies style.

I simply told her, "I need one of the larger tables. Wherever you have to get it from is all right with me." When she protested that she'd been doing this for years and the table that I had would work fine. I countered with, "I think you'd rather make that adjustment now, rather than wait for the woman who's footing the bills for this event to ask you to make that change. And trust me, she's going to want me to be accommodated—she's an author just like me. Please find me the right table."

So I was already a little on heat because the table incident put my skirt in the dirt. So I wasn't in the best of spirits when that same venue representative decided to plop a sprawling display of fashion racks and a boutique vendor directly next to the signing table. Seriously? Why don't you block me from all sides? The vendor asked if it was all right if she could put her clothes between my table and hers—taking up the rest of the small amount of space left. I quickly explained, "I would appreciate it if you put the clothes on the *opposite* side of your table. I need to keep this side clear." And I left it at that.

My son froze in the middle of pulling the books out of the boxes and placing them on table and said, "Mom, you sounded like a lawyer."

And given the fact that I worked for lawyers and some of them didn't have the best reputation, all I could say was, "Really?"

To which my Road Doll said in a taunting tone—her kind of haughty tone, "*I'm* the featured author around here. *I'm* the star. No you don't try to take over my territory." (Or something along those lines.).

I was shocked, because that's not what I thought was in my consciousness; but it very well could have been in my subconscious mind and that's the way it came out. And if there is any one of my people who could know it when they heard it—could spot it if I've got it—my Road Doll could. Because at one time, before she evolved into the more patient, compassionate, loving woman she is now, I used to hear it from her more often than I would like. Sometimes I don't even think she realizes that she's hurt me. There was one point I had to learn to accept the apology that would never come.

That was the time I was grieving over the loss of my Tony and she, and my other Road Doll, Mari, took me to my favorite restaurant to cheer me up. During the dinner a statement was made about Tony, and though it might have been true, it didn't need to be said at that time.

And it certainly didn't need to be said in the manner that she had. It hurt. Bad. And it took me years to say something to her about it and to mention how much it hurt. Truthfully, her response when I finally managed to bring it to her attention was to blow it off with another flip statement. Like I said, I had to learn to accept the apology that would never come, because she didn't see anything wrong with what she said, no matter how much it hurt me.

So that being said, if *she* was also calling me out at the author brunch on something I spoke out of pocket, then I definitely did not sound like an enlightened person; it did not sound like a person who embraces Christ Consciousness.

I stood from the table, aiming to apologize. By this time they had moved the vendor somewhere else. My son said I should wait until after the lady finished putting all of her items out. My Road Doll cut in and said, "She might be feeling some kind of way right about now. And it'll go a long way to getting her to all right before the event starts if you say something right now."

I waited for a point in between what they both wanted, when she was almost done, and then went over to the woman and said, "Do you have a minute?"

She grimaced at first and I realize she thought I was going to say something else that was worse than before. That pained me. "I said, I have my conscious with me," I gestured toward J. L. and Deb. "And they pointed out the fact that what I said to you wasn't right. I apologize for the way it sounded; and I certainly didn't mean for them to move you. I truly, truly apologize for being mean or that I offended you in any kind of way."

That woman's face lit up like it was Christmas. She pulled me in for a hug and said, "Thank you for acknowledging it. You didn't have to apologize, but thank you. Thank you."

Simple. Done deal. That's all she needed to put that pep back in her step; to make her feel all right again—because my negative vibration *had* affected her. And after I apologized, she wouldn't stop talking to my people or trying to get my attention on things for the rest of the event. She even sent some folks directly from her table to mine. All was forgiven and I felt lighter; much better—because I was back into who I truly was after recognizing and dealing with that momentary lapse into a place I never like to travel—ego.

And on another note, let me give you a current update. My Road Doll read the manuscript for this book (nothing goes to print without her putting eyes on it first), and she read this part. She immediately sent an email with an apology, and then we talked right after. She's in a different space than when she first made that statement, and even the eight years later when I brought it to her awareness. Somehow reading it here, in this format, was able to express more than I had been able before. So, while I had already "accepted the apology that I would never receive", it's a wonderful feeling for the person who I know, in my heart of hearts, doesn't have intentions to hurt me—had finally acknowledged that she had. Sometimes, we have to weigh out a person's importance in our lives. Was that one incident enough for me to end our friendship. No? She had enough skin in the game that I could absorbed

Equally, I strive to work on not hurting people in words and deeds. When someone brings it to my attention that I have done so, I don't hesitate to apologize. I wait until later to analyze what transpired, and how I could have done things differently where it got to a point that the other person felt slighted or hurt. I don't wish that on anyone. I know how it feels when little hurts linger for too long. They're almost as damaging as "big ones". Why? Because sometimes the thought is, "this is such a small thing. I should be able to get over it." But it stays there in the back of your mind.

Little things "staying in the back of the mind" might also another reason that I won't lose family or friends over money. When someone comes with a request, I never give more than I can afford to lose. If someone asks for $500, I might shell out $50 to $100. They can't say that I didn't help them, but it also stops a trend of making me the first place they turn when they haven't worked their financial issues out. Truthfully, I give it as a gift so that it relieves the pressure of having to return anything. They may have every good intention, but life might come between them and the ability to pay you back. That way, they know that I've helped them, and I don't end up angry when that money doesn't come back my way. Or feel some kind of way when I see their name pop up on my phone. No, I am *not* going to lose people over money. Period.

There are people in your life who are there as a barometer for where you are in life. My circle, which I shared with you earlier, is pretty small. They are not "yes" people. They are people who give it to me straight, no chaser. Even my son. Sometimes it's amazing hearing him throw my own words back at me in an effort to get me to see a point.

That night, I sold the majority of the books that was on the table— because the vibration from that exchange carried into what I did from that point on. Lesson learned.

Get it in Writing

The family drama with Tee and Sister Aridell stems from a real life incident on my Facebook page. I posted a picture that had been taken in Atlanta a year before. I was sitting in a comfortable chair, wearing a cool pair of shades, spread out in a pose that said, "Just chillin'". Something about that image incensed the maternal aunt of my niece (I'm the aunt on the father's side). So when she posted the words:

"Your great nethew (that's the way she spelled it several times in our conversation) passed & I didn't see you at his service this past Saturday nor anyone else representing the Woodson family!"

The fact that she did this in a public forum, meant that I needed to address it in that very same public forum. It wasn't the most pleasant of exchanges that I've had in a while. You've already read the majority of it—how I didn't see the post about the child's death or the funeral, etc., so I won't go over it again. I'm only writing this to share one valuable piece of information that has saved my bacon and my eggs on a number of occasions.

The Living Arrangement Contract. The one that my niece, Tee, and her mother both refused to sign before she would be allowed to come live with me. Now I'm all for taking in family, but setting some boundaries are key. And putting it in writing? Priceless! Then people can't say, "Oh, I forgot." "I didn't know." "You never said that." "I didn't agree to that." Bull. You read it and signed it. Or didn't, which means you don't get to walk through my door. And life goes on.

Well, given the fact my niece was giving her mother so many problems at that time, and living with me was the best option, the contract for both of them to sign stated the rules, conditions, and expectations of living under my roof. It covered:

What chores she was expected to handle and when
Curfew times for weekdays and weekends
Respecting my space and personal things
Not having strange folks all up in my house
Private school attendance and the kind of grades she was to bring in (a "C" was fine, if it was an honest "C" and not her b.s'ing on getting her work done)
No profanity
Conducting herself like she had some sense
Respect for her mother, all adults and me
Going to church every Sunday (didn't have to be *my* church) (Oh, and I wasn't as much of a heathen back then)
Dating boys under my watch would happen she was damn near 50

It also had the items that I would provide and pay for:
Private School
Extracurricular activities
Food
New clothing when it was earned
Special events/trips when it was earned

There's more, but I believe this was the gist of everything.

They arrived at my house with my niece's personal items all packed in suitcases. I gave them both a copy of the Living Arrangement Contract to read. And they went left. Big time.

Well, if you can't abide by my rules, looks like y'all are back to square one. And they were. The mother was under the impression that the contract would interfere with those child support checks she received from my brother. Even though the contract would only be known between the three of us and I would be paying everything out of my own pocket. The child, though, realized, "Auntie Lissa don't play and I'm not going to be able to run over her like I'm doing to mom" and was not feeling it. Fine by me. Take your little munchkin right back home. And that's exactly what happened. Didn't hear a peep from either one of them for a looooooong time.

There's something about putting things on paper and having people commit to them that changes the whole dynamic of things. And that's fine. Personally, some children work better when they know what's expected rather than guessing at it or being able to manipulate their way out of things.

I highly recommend a living arrangement contract for pre-teens, teens or even grown children returning to the fold. Why? When it's in writing people can't embrace amnesia when things aren't done.

That's my parenting tip for today. Carry on.

Let it Go

My nephew and I end up as partners quite often on Sundays when I came over to play Bid at his grandmother's house where I learned to play the game. And it brightened my day on the night that he exclaimed after a particularly good run and we ran several sets of partners off the table, "No one comes between me and my Auntie. Y'all gon' learn t'day."

Well someone did try—and it came out of nowhere. The night of my nephew's maternal aunt's funeral, I came over to play cards with them. His sister Deena received a text that said, "Do you know who Lissa is?" She turned the screen to my nephew. I looked at my nephew across the table and knew that trouble was brewing. His mouth tightened and he had this murderous look in his eyes. He showed me that text.

There was a room full of people, some watching the table, waiting their turn to play cards, others were eating some of the food spread out on the counter; the rest had their eyes glued to television. All of them totally unaware of the tension on the room. I picked up my phone and though DeMarco was sitting right across from me, I sent him a text that said, "You know what's about to happen, right?"

Let me put it in context. I am related to my nephew by blood, and his sister—by love. I have never treated them any different. From what I understand, my brother, because of an incident with DeMarco's mother's ex-boyfriend, had reason to believe that my nephew wasn't actually his child. So after the ex put a warning gunshot at my brother, my brother has had nothing to do with my nephew since age five. I only found out my brother's truth when I finally called him on his non-involvement about a year after DeMarco had been back in my life. Regardless, what my nephew believes is equally as important. I love them both, so I can't call it either way, and I don't need to. My son and I have been the only people from our side of the spectrum to interact with DeMarco or any of my other nieces and nephews that have a relationship with me. So the story would continue to be told: Deena and DeMarco had the "same father". Now, because their cousin was upset after finding out that none of the money from his mother's estate would land in his pockets—he sought to hurt his family by revealing my true identity to Deena.

My nephew went outside with me to talk. I told him, "She would appreciate hearing it from you than hearing it maliciously from him."

All of a sudden, at 2:37 a.m. people were on the phone calling each other; getting approval, afraid of Deena's reaction to the truth. I left around 3:30 in the morning and the last thing I saw in my rearview mirror was my nephew escorting Deena out of her van and walking her back toward the house.

I cried all the way home. DeMarco had already lost one of his girlfriends because of me—one who believed he was calling me "Auntie" as a cover for something else.

My nephew loves women. Correction—my nephew loves *mature* women. So when I reappeared on the scene last year, it caused a major problem with his current girlfriend who was hell bent on knowing *how* we were related. Especially since she already knew everyone of importance in his family. At the time, because no one wanted Deena to find out the truth, no one would tell the girlfriend how I actually fit into the family line. The current girlfriend actually began to think that I was his *new girlfriend.* Come to find out, I *am* in the age bracket he likes to date and he generally tends to attract strong Black women. So thinking this new person, a middle-aged woman that suddenly appears at his grandmother's home wasn't a stretch. One of the (minor) reasons they broke up was that she believed he was lying—using the word "Auntie" as a cover. No matter how long they'd been together, the girlfriend didn't really now my nephew. He doesn't lie, and he keeps his stuff all above board with all of his women.

My nephew's family had embraced may son and me as if those "missing" years where we had lost touch. So the last thing I wanted to do was to be a cause of pain or dissension within the family. I already had very little interaction with some members of my biological family to begin with. I choose who I want to be my family among people I trust all the way down to my soul.

I received a text from DeMarco two hours later that read, "She already knew."

Now here it is, everyone thought *they* were keeping me a secret from her, and Deena was actually keeping a secret from *them*. She told everyone after I left, "I don't want to talk about it anymore. She's my auntie. That's it and that's all."

I found it amazing though; that she and I had already connected on a loving level. She would drop everything to come to one of my gatherings. Now she wanted to learn how to play Bid Whist when all the years before she hadn't bothered. She eventually got to the point: "No, I'm riding with Auntie Lissa." / "No, we're going to do what Auntie Lissa said do." / "I only feel comfortable playing Bid with Auntie Lissa" (probably because I encourage to go with her gut and not to be afraid. I don't want her to take as long as I did to get to that point.) When their mother came to me once and said, "thank you," because of the way I handled things with her daughter; I thought, *Don't thank me, that's what any decent human being would do.*

Family secrets don't always stay secret. Amazing how that person who sent my niece that text, had meant to cause even more pain to his loved ones at a time they were grieving the loss of someone special; Amazing how everyone believed it would be such a horrible thing if

Deena knew the truth. Instead, what he had done was free everyone from the burden of secrecy they'd been under for over twenty years; the always having to watch what was said; the back peddling when something actually slipped.

What the man had done was sealed it for me that love trumps all. And when Deena hugged me the next time I saw her; she said that she loved me so very much, all I could think was, "Boston."

The Art of Allowing

My true mother is still with the woman she seduced almost a fifteen ago. The woman was twenty years younger (my mother was over sixty at the time. Told you she had skills.) She and this woman embarked on a relationship that was wonderful at times, but tumultuous at best. Mind you, I was the one who introduced them, though not for *that* reason, but hey …

Later the lover was angered that I put the brakes on my finances which was funding their romance. They were having a good run. A *very* good run. But I had to tighten ship, since having my finances together was important to me. My mother's lover gave me the cold shoulder for a long time after that.

But here's what I find interesting. My mother keeps falling for straight women who loved her personality, sense of humor, the pleasure she brings, but not the stigma that comes along with a homosexual relationship. My biological mother was the same way. She denied her nature as much as possible; but had enjoyed the intimate part of being with my true mother so much, that she … hmmm, how do I put this delicately? She introduced a few family members to the experience.

Now, here it is thirty-plus years later and my true mother is with another woman, who because of religious reasons, does not want their relationship to be out in the open. Their lie is easy to manage because my true mother is so much older then her. On the surface, it seems that her mate is strictly a caretaker. Every time the minister of this particular religion her lover has been involved in speaks out against homosexuality; the lover shuts off and pushes my mother away; blaming her for turning her into something she shouldn't be.

I won't mention that after the first intimate experience with my true mother; the lover left her home, her husband, and her son in the city and moved into my house with my true mother in the 'burbs.

Now for the hard part. The woman was just as emotionally abusive as my biological mother had been—maybe even more, because my true mother was older and certainly, more vulnerable. I had to wonder, how in the hell did my true mother keep attracting this same scenario into her life? First my bio mom, who became angry, bitter and unfulfilled when she ended the intimate parts of their relationship the moment religion and judgment dropped in for a visit and stayed far past their welcome.

Then my true mother fell for another younger woman who loved her, but was too afraid to act on what she felt so they never got together. And then the current one, who at first played the kind of games that would've made the average person kick her to the curb; all because she's still ashamed of being in love with a woman. This is where I learned the true meaning of when you don't get the lesson, The Creator/Universe continues to bring the same lesson in many forms.

Saying anything about the relationship, or trying to intervene was not the way to go. At one point, when they finally moved into another place, my true mother even felt uncomfortable having me over their house because her lover was still so angry with me. That really hurt and felt abandoned all over again. Then my true mother decided to get her own place in a senior citizens building. That worked well, until the lover made the decision to rent a house in the 'burbs. I pleaded with my true mother not to give up her place since it was inexpensive and decent and having her own was best. I wasn't saying for her not to move in with the woman; only that she needed to keep her own place as well. She didn't listen, and ended up regretting it at several points.

My true mother ended up in the hospital and then long-term rehab. This woman, because of her commitments to her place of worship, didn't come as often as she should. I was a little upset, but I had to realize that this is the path my true mother chose. I had no right to interfere with her lesson. But that was easier said than done.

The doctors felt it best for her to remain in rehab; but somehow my true mother, maneuvered her way back home—wanting to be with her mate. When it became obvious that the people in said home could barely take care of themselves, and they dropped her while trying to get her over to a chair, I made the calls to the hospital administrator to get her back into the long-term care facility. The ambulance came and scooped her up. Then, once again, my mother messed up the best-laid plans where she ended up back at home.

Many times I thought about taking over completely—but the issue would remain. If I moved her away from her lover, I think she would've died a lot sooner than if I let her remain.

My true mother was comfortable in that space; wanted to stay close to her lady love—even though, with her being bed-ridden, they couldn't be as intimate as they once were. (Although, the lover still shares a sly smile with my true mother from time to time, so … "bedridden" doesn't mean "not capable").

Knowing that everyone—doctors, nurses said she should be in rehab, but my mother constantly rallied against it, I finally had to tell myself, it wouldn't be me laying up in that hospital surrounded by strangers, waiting for people to come see me everyday, staring at a television that wouldn't even have the cooking shows. So, I stopped fighting a battle she didn't want me to win. She came here with a certain lessons that were part of her spiritual journey.

Even though it hurt, I stopped fighting a battle I *couldn't* win. I was standing in the way of her lesson. I'm telling you that had to be the hardest thing for me to grasp—allowing people to travel their path. I'm a take charge kind of woman; a fix-it kind of woman; and seeing anyone

I love in pain or in trouble, brings out a side of me that won't back down until everything is all right in their world again.

Now, I take the passenger seat instead. I might hold their map, look at the direction they're going in, and offer a shortcut or a better route to get there, but the one thing I won't do is jump into the driver seat of their car and take over the entire trip.

This act of "allowing" covers family, friends, co-workers, associates and total strangers. When we "effort" over something in another person's life; we are actually interfering with their life's lessons. When people keep experiencing the same things over and over again; that's a true sign that there's a lesson that's unfolding; and somehow, some way; the person(s) involved aren't getting it. It's not our job to make sure they do. The Creator is perfectly capable of handling things with no help from us.

Let's take children for instance, though this can apply to all relationships. As parents, we're concerned about them. And as a parent, there are times we've been up and down the same road with them on certain things. At some point, realization kicks in that we're fighting a battle that even they, however misguided it is, do not want us to win. The most we can do is make sure that they know that we love them unconditionally. *Unconditionally.* And that means even though they might not give back what we give them, (and it might never be an even exchange), we will love them still. They need to know that. *At least that.* And say it enough for it to sink into their subconscious mind.

Parents can guide, talk to they're blue in the face; but ultimately, children are going to follow the path of their own lessons or inwardly resent anyone who forces them to go against their own goals and desires.

On another note, try not to hold them to "your expectations" or see the missed opportunities that you laid out for them as something that makes them not quite the people you believe they could have been. Though there might be some truth in the fact that you, in your wisdom and experience, might have great insight. Accept that it's not the path that was for them.

Meet them at their level. One day, they'll meet you at yours.

Life is in Your Favor

I was in T. J. Maxx downtown on State Street buying some new items for that deluxe apartment on Olgesby where I lived at the time. A thought had crossed my mind: you know, it probably wasn't fair that I got that apartment when the property manager had said, "there are people on the waiting list; there were people who had a deposit on that apartment, but if you want it, it's yours…" I was about to go into guilt mode. I never want things to come to me at the expense of others.

I hadn't put that thought out there for a split-second, when this strange lady in front of me in line, turns around and puts her hand on my arm and says, "Favor ain't always fair."

I froze, but I had to ask, "What did you just say to me?"

She repeated, "Favor ain't always fair."

I fell silent.

Favor, isn't always fair.

Back then, those were the words that I needed to hear to release the guilt that I felt at times when things happened for me, but didn't happen for others.

It's the same thing that made me feel some kind of way on the cruise ship when the Chef de Cuisine and his whole line came out to apologize for an error that was made with my food—an error that could have made the cruise all about me being in one particular room for the rest of those days. It wasn't their actions that caused me to feel a little guilt; it was the response from others around me that did.

"The Queen." A woman loves to be called that, but not necessarily when others see it as taking away something from themselves; like they are lacking in some way. *She ain't nobody. She's just like me. Why is she getting something that I'm not? What's wrong with me?" What did she do to deserve all that special treatment?*

Well, I don't think the people at my table realized it, but the *entire table* was served before anyone else in our huge group. Every single meal service. They only saw that I, only a sub-level, was served before them. They were too busy noticing what was happening for me, and not how everything panned out for everyone at the table. I thought that was interesting. Having those two extra staff put at the table for me (ones who had been made abreast of every single ingredient of selections on the menu so that another mistake wouldn't happen), freed the regular servers up to take care of the five of them.

All of a sudden the dinner portions of everyone at my table were larger than it was at other tables. We finished our meals long before other tables in the area, even when we arrived late. But they didn't notice any of that. "If The Queen isn't happy, *nobody's* happy." They meant it to be sarcastic and at first it put a damper on what was given to me as a gift for what could've put me knee deep on the porcelain throne for days. My response to the chef's efforts was total acceptance and embracing him—not going into "sista girl" mode and letting them have it with both barrels and a side order of "neck rock".

Before I let their words put a taint to the dinner part of the cruise experience—I began to accept their words. The Queen. All right, let me stop feeling bad about things and roll with that.

Soon, I was able to laugh when they pointed things out; and I would respond by pointing out the ways that benefitted them that they weren't seeing. By Day two, the way they said, "The Queen" didn't have quite the same bite as it did the first day. And what's really funny is that they started acting as if they were Queens, too (making requests that were totally off the menu, having seconds, sometimes thirds of a particular item; ordering more than one of a particular course—keeping the servers busy). I found it to be humorous. When I began to accept what had been bestowed on me; others began to be comfortable with it as well.

Same with making the decision to wear Sister Locs. When I first allowed the locticians to put them in, I still wore a wig out in public. Why? Because I wasn't comfortable with my natural hair. I'd been in wig, weaves, braids, sew-ins—you name it, I've had it. But there was something about my natural hair that made me less comfortable, as though I would be judged negatively in some way. I felt that folks at the conservative law firm where I worked would not be pleased.

Finally, at one point, I looked in the mirror and said, "You know what? I'm wearing my hair. I don't care what anyone thinks." I snatched off that wig, wore my short locs as though I believed I looked like a million bucks.

Do you know what happened? I received more compliments on my natural hair than when I had all that other stuff up on my head!! White people, Asian people, Latina, and definitely the sisters—everyone loved my new look. Said it took years off.

When I became comfortable with how I looked, then so did everyone else.

So while I'm working on the outside of me—changing my eating habits, exercise, dancing, volleyball, walking, 96-ounces of water per day; I also realize the need to continue working on the inside of me. I'm constantly evolving, checking my thought processes, seeing what and how I could have handled a situation or a person better. It's a never-ending process. A daily process. I strive, always, to become a better me.

To end this book, I'm sharing a few of the affirmations that I've used and then one last short story about my nephew:

Thank you that I am allowing others to have their life experiences, and I support them fully in their process. I am totally at peace and non-judgmental with their path and outcomes

Thank you for more loving and harmonious relationships in all aspects of my life

Thank you that my body is slimming down, releasing excess pounds and inches in ease comfort and joy under grace and in a perfect way. Exercising and dancing is easy and effortless and my metabolism speeds up to accommodate this desire

Thank you that I receive lots of money and abundance from expected and unexpected sources on a daily basis; I Am experiencing a superabundance of prosperity and people to help me, places, things, and events, money substance and health of my projects and myself.

Thank you that my old/outstanding accounts payable/bills/debts to people and companies are paid in full at very little or no cost to me, under grace and in a perfect way

I love my physical body, my cells, my atoms, my molecules, my lymphatic system, my digestive system, my circulatory system, my nervous system, my brain, my heart, my organs, my emotional body, my spiritual body, my mind, and my connection to The Creator.

And this is a little of what I wrote when I asked The Creator for a mate: I Am experiencing a wonderful, harmonious, peaceful and balanced intimate relationship where I am protected, cherished and loved by a man who protects my heart, mind and body, who comforts and uplifts me; who is adventurous, spontaneous, focused, supportive, compassionate, inclusive, sharing, giving, fair, complementary, trusting and trustworthy.

Set Yourself Up For Success

One Friday night around eight, my nephew, DeMarco, called and said, "Auntie, come out and play with me."

He wanted me to go to a place I now call "The Shark Tank" — a spot on 64th & Stony Island where a group of seasoned card players get together to play Bid Whist, chow down, listen to good music and have a great time. My initial reaction was, "No." Those people had been playing for years—they were tournament players. At the time, I was nowhere near their league. Well, he twisted my arm, forcing me to go after saying, "Come on. Just for an hour, Auntie."

We came through the door kicking tail and taking names. We arrived at nine, but didn't get up from that first table until midnight. And that was because another team finally beat us. He walked me over to the buffet table and fixed me a plate. We ate and were back down at another table. I forgot all about that "only 1 hour" I was supposed to be there.

For the most part, I had let DeMarco take the lead in playing all night long—because I was intimidated and afraid to fail. But I finally landed a hand that was so dynamic, that I was afraid *not* to bid. My nephew would've never let me live it down if I had passed on a hand like that. So, I bid a six low to take out a five no trump. Bid players understand that's a smart move. There were actually two gaps in my spread that I knew would land me in trouble. We played out the hand, and when I entered the "trouble" zone my nephew whipped out the cards that mattered.

When the last book turned, DeMarco jumped up from the table and yelled, "Six, No trump. Boston. And she did it by her damn self." (Actually, I couldn't have done it without him, but I took his meaning). All of a sudden, people in the room—about fifty spread out at about six tables and a couple of sofas—applauded. I smiled, though I didn't understand why there would have been a reason for them to do that—my kind of win happened for them all the time.

But it was my nephew being proud of me that did it for them and me. After that, I started bidding more and more—making most, losing a few. But I had the will to try. I released the fear of not being good enough. I released my normal way of embracing failure first, then found that jumping into the deep end wasn't as bad as I thought it would be.

Pull out a few sheets of paper. Write down the negative experiences-past and present—that have impacted you the most. One line each will suffice. Right next to those experiences, write a single word or words to describe what you were feeling at the time. After you're done, pull out another sheet of paper and rewrite those experiences into a positive affirmation.

If one experience made you angry, you might write something like. I Am experiencing an overabundance of joy (or happiness).

Do this for every single experience. There might be some duplicates, but remember to write the affirmations in present tense—by starting it with I Am experiencing.

Today is your Independence Day. Why not declare your independence from the things that might be holding you captive? It is equally important that you undertake the journey for spiritual, physical, mental and emotional health as well. By stating your personal affirmations you create yourself, in the morning and right before you go to bed, soon you'll be able to feel a sense of peace as you release yourself along with everyone and everything involved.

As me how I know.

Naleighna Kai

is a Chicago native, is an inspirational speaker, a Mercedes Benz Mentor Award Nominee, the national bestselling author of *Every Woman Needs a Wife, Open Door Marriage, Was it Good For You Too?*, co-author of *Speak it into Existence* with Sesvalah, and a contributing author to a *New York Times* bestseller. She started writing in December of 1999, self-publishing her first three novels before landing a book deal with an imprint of Simon & Schuster and then a deal with an independent publishing house founded by two national bestselling authors.

Naleighna is the CEO of Macro Marketing & Promotions Group, as well as marketing consultant to several national bestselling authors and a publishing consultant to aspiring writers. She is the mother of J. L. Woodson, the NAACP Image Award Nominee She is currently working on her next novels, *Slaves of Heaven* and *Mercury Sunrise*.

* * *

www.naleighnakai.com
www.thecavalcadeofauthors.com
Facebook: Naleighna Kai
Twitter: @naleighnakai

other novels by Naleighna Kai

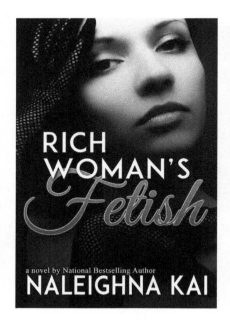

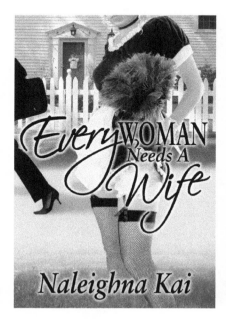

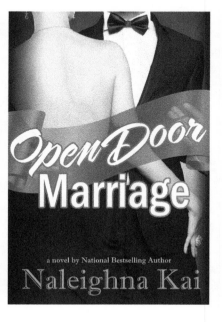